An Orchid in my Belly Button
First published in Great Britain by Elsewhen Press, 2025
An imprint of Alnpete Limited

Copyright © Katy Wimhurst, 2025. All rights reserved
The right of Katy Wimhurst to be identified as the author of this work has been asserted in accordance with sections 77 and 78 of the Copyright, Designs and Patents Act 1988. No part of this publication may be reproduced, scanned, stored in a retrieval system or transmitted in any form, or by any means (electronic, mechanical, telepathic, magical, or otherwise) without the prior written permission of the copyright owner. No part of this book may be used or reproduced in any manner for the purpose of training artificial intelligence technologies or systems. In accordance with Article 4(3) of the Digital Single Market Directive 2019/790, Elsewhen Press expressly reserves this work from the text and data mining exception.

'Snow on Snow' was first published in *Cafe Irreal*, #88, August 2023. 'The Woman with Birds In Her Hair' won the Writers' Forum short story competition and was published in *Writers Forum Magazine*, October 2022. 'The Carp Whisperer,' was co-written by Petra McQueen and first published in *Tempest*, 2019, Patrician Press. 'The Blind Ark' was first published in *Shooterlit* #54, 2018. 'Ms Wiffle's Open Book' was first published in *WriteNight Anthology*, 2021, Patrician Press. 'Bootleg Chocolate' was first published in *Epoque Magazine* #12, 2022. 'The Mushroom Lovers' was first published in *Cafe Irreal* #90, May 2024. 'The Shaman of Smog' won the Earlyworks short story competition, 2018, published in *The Sorcery of Smog*, 2018, Earlyworks Press. 'Calmer Karma' was first published in *DogVersusSandwich*, May 2009. The page 1 Isaiah quote is from the World English Bible (British) translation.

Elsewhen Press, PO Box 757, Dartford, Kent DA2 7TQ
www.elsewhen.press

British Library Cataloguing in Publication Data.
A catalogue record for this book is available from the British Library.

ISBN 978-1-915304-69-8 Print edition
ISBN 978-1-915304-79-7 eBook edition

Condition of Sale
This book is sold subject to the condition that it shall not, by way of trade or otherwise, be lent, re-sold, hired out or otherwise circulated in any form of binding or cover other than that in which it is published and without a similar condition including this condition being imposed on the subsequent purchaser.

This book is copyright under the Berne Convention.
Elsewhen Press & Planet-Clock Design are trademarks of Alnpete Limited

Designed and formatted by Elsewhen Press

This book is a work of fiction. All names, characters, places, organisations, and events are either a product of the author's fertile imagination or are used fictitiously. Any resemblance to actual events, corporations, places or people (living, dead, or floral) is purely coincidental.

Band-Aid is a trademark of KENVUE INC.; Barbie is a trademark of Mattel, Inc.; Barclays Bank is a trademark of Barclays Plc; Beatles is a trademark of Apple Corps Limited; Blur is a trademark of Blur (a partnership); BMW is a trademark of Bayerische Motoren Werke Aktiengesellschaft; Boden is a trademark of J.P. Boden & Co Ltd; Caffe Nero is a trademark of Italian Coffee Holdings Ltd; Calvin Klein is a trademark of Calvin Klein Trademark Trust; Channel 4 is a trademark of Channel Four Television Corporation; Citizen's Advice Bureau is a trademark of The National Association of Citizens Advice Bureaux; Classic FM is a trademark of Classic FM Limited; Co-op is a trademark of Co-operative Group Limited; Dangermouse is a trademark of Boat Rocker Rights, Inc.; DM is a trademark of Dr Martens International Trading GmbH; Dr Who, Gardeners' World, Radio 2, and Radio 4 are trademarks of The British Broadcasting Corporation; eBay is a trademark of eBay Inc.; Eden Project is a trademark of The Eden Trust; Estee Lauder is a trademark of Estee Lauder Cosmetics Limited; Facebook is a trademark of Meta Platforms, Inc.; Fraggle Rock is a trademark of The Jim Henson Company, Inc; Goldsmiths is a trademark of Goldsmiths College; Google is a trademark of Google LLC; H&M is a trademark of H & M Hennes & Mauritz AB; Hello! is a trademark of HOLA S.L.; Henry is a trademark of Numatic International Limited; Hobnob is a trademark of PLADIS (UK) LIMITED; Instagram is a trademark of Instagram, LLC; iPad is a trademark of APPLE INC.; KitKat is a trademark of Société des Produits Nestlé S.A.; Kung Fu Panda is a trademark of DreamWorks Animation L.L.C.; Lynx is a trademark of Unilever Global IP Limited; Maybelline is a trademark of L'Oréal; Minecraft is a trademark of Microsoft Corporation; Netflix is a trademark of Netflix, Inc.; Next is a trademark of Next Retail Limited; Nirvana, and Smells like Teen Spirit are trademarks of Nirvana L.L.C.; Poundland is a trademark of Poundland Limited; Radiohead is a trademark of Radiohead Trademark Limited; Scooby-Doo is a trademark of Hanna-Barbera Productions, Inc.; Sky news is a trademark of Sky Limited; Stamford Bridge is a trademark of Chelsea Football Club Limited; Taylor Swift is a trademark of TAS Rights Management, LLC; Tesco and Tesco Express are trademarks of Tesco Stores Limited; The Evening Standard is a trademark of Evening Standard Limited; The Grinch is a trademark of Dr. Seuss Enterprises, L.P.; The Guardian is a trademark of Guardian News & Media Limited; The Telegraph is a trademark of Telegraph Media Group Holdings Limited; Urban Species is a trademark of Urban Species Retail Limited; Vogue is a trademark of The Conde Nast Publications Limited. Use of trademarks has not been authorised, sponsored, or otherwise approved by the trademark owners.

Contents

An Orchid in my Belly Button 1
Nothing Like Ice Cream in the Apocalypse 5
Snow on Snow 15
The Ghosts of Crabs 17
The Woman with Birds in Her Hair 25
Vanity Vines 35
The Carp Whisperer 45
Existential Shrug 55
The Art of Rubbish 63
The Mushroom Lovers 73
Ms Wiffle's Open Book 77
Bootleg Chocolate 83
Fox Freak 91
The Blind Ark 103
The Shaman of Smog 119
Calmer Karma 129
Family, Fungi, Friends 131
Butterflies and a Gun 143
Everything Sucks 153

For Ann Wimhurst

AN ORCHID IN MY BELLY BUTTON

'You will be like a watered garden.'
Isaiah 58:11

I find the first one while on the toilet—a daisy stuck to my inner thigh, its petals closed. I must have picked it up in the garden. When I try to pluck it off, my skin tugs and I feel a twinge of pain. It can't be sprouting from me, can it? Holding the stalk between fingertip and thumb, I pull it again gently and my mouth drops open in disbelief.

Back outside, my mind is hazy. I sit down and slip my hand under my skirt to touch the thing once more. Still there. Am I now one percent flower? A buoyant feeling slowly unfurls, like sap rising.

The wooden fence encloses the small garden on three sides. I have planted it so that flowers bloom all year; now the beds are spilling with fleabane, lavender, scabious, marjoram, and borage. I lie down, stretch my arms out like branches, and close my eyes. My head instinctively turns towards the sun.

Later that day, the presence of my daisy makes me bold enough to open the utility bills I've been avoiding. What else can I cut besides cancelling my subscription to *Gardeners' World* and my annual visit to the Eden Project in Cornwall to get away from everything? I let out a breath and then log in to check my student loan balance, too. That night, sleep doesn't come easily and my finger keeps reaching for the daisy.

On Saturday, another daisy budding next to the original lifts my heart. I have been wearing skirts, not wanting to flatten the flower against jeans, and I take care to walk with my feet wider apart than normal.

'Why are you waddling?' asks my friend Amy, when she drops in for a cup of tea.

'Quack.' I laugh off the comment. Some things are more magical if left a secret.

On Monday, a slight prickle on my toes alerts me to

tiny green shoots appearing there. I crouch to inspect them. What might this be? Should I visit a doctor? Or a botanist? Are there people versed in both fields? Still, I don't feel alarmed by my foliage. Maybe this is who—or what—I really am.

The following day, hundreds of verdant shoots cover the top of both feet, a contrast with my flat's faux-oak vinyl floor. By Thursday, the grass is a few centimetres long, so I trim it with scissors to fit into footwear. I go barefoot at home, but when I venture out, boots hide the plants without harming them.

'Curious fashion statement.' My boss stares at the Wellingtons beneath my linen dress.

I chuckle; humour people and they don't pry. Fortunately, my work—which bores me—can be done from home. I take that option, deciding to come into the office only once each month.

Two days later, I wake to see ivy toadflax sprouting along my collarbones. I shiver with delight.

It isn't just my body that is changing. Usually an inveterate worrier, my anxieties dissipate like dandelion seeds in the wind. I ignore Channel 4 News, which I typically follow, and sleep more soundly. I stop eating pizza and toast, having the urge to snack on vegetables and salads instead.

My dad phones. 'Hello stranger.'

'Hi Dad. Sorry. I've been busy.'

'How's work?'

'Oh, you know…'

'You should have been a solicitor like your sister.'

'So you say. How are things?'

He launches into a moan about the tensions at his golf club. After ten minutes, I make an excuse and end the call, wishing there was one family member to whom I could relate.

The next morning, a wild orchid is growing out of my belly button. Smiling, I glide a fingertip lightly over its soft cream petals. My feet and calves are now carpeted in grass, which I trim every couple of days. I leave the curtains drawn at the front of the flat and stroll around naked, relishing the sensation of grass blades tickling my skin. A bumble bee buzzes after me like an eager lover; I imagine it pollinating my plants.

My ex emails, saying he thinks about me all the time and is still sorry. I remember him banging on about the climate crisis and leaving half-drunk mugs of rosehip tea everywhere; recall, too, finding the texts from the other woman. Distress crawling up me like a caterpillar, I delete the email.

A week later, lobelia cascades through my long dark hair, ivy branches up both arms, and a fern spills from my ear. I twist my head to examine my back in the mirror. A wildflower meadow sprouts there; grasses, clover, cornflowers, and poppies, attended by three peacock butterflies. I stretch my hands up in a gesture of exaltation. 'I'm Mother Nature.'

I wake one morning to find a blackbird sleeping on my chest. When I sit up, it chitters in fright. 'Calm down,' I whisper, but it flits freely out of the window I've left open. I get up and the soles of my feet prickle as I walk. Tiny roots are growing from them.

Two days later, the roots are ten centimetres long, making it hard to move around. *It's time,* I think. The Earth is calling, a promise of escape and enchantment. I spend hours in the garden; the roots needle down, bonding me to the soil.

Night follows day follows night. I haven't shifted from outside. My thoughts settle and slow until my mind is empty, aware only of shifting light and shadow; of warm sun and cool moon.

NOTHING LIKE ICE CREAM IN THE APOCALYPSE

Hilda couldn't recall putting the three old toasters on the shelf in her tiny spare bedroom, though she was getting forgetful at her age. *The mystery of the toasters.*

Outside Whittington Park later, she came across four rusty bikes dumped, each with only one wheel. Hilda visited the city park daily to walk off the stiffness in her knees. She couldn't help staring at the damaged vehicles and recalling the toasters. The June sun painted sharp outlines of the things on the brick wall behind.

Maddy, a local friend of similar age who was exiting the park, stopped by Hilda and peered at the bikes, too. She lived in a posh Georgian house on a nearby street and had an accent to match. 'No one's going to get far on those.'

'Except unicyclists,' said Hilda with a chuckle.

'Seriously, people who fly-tip should be fined.'

'You know, I've never got that phrase,' said Hilda. 'No flies around these bikes. I only tip waiters or taxi drivers, not bugs.'

'You say the wackiest things.'

Hilda was often told that. She didn't try self-consciously to be offbeat, but she prided herself on her candour.

Two days later, Hilda bumped into Maddy once more in Whittington Park. Seven red Henry vacuum cleaners had been left just inside the cast-iron gates, and teenagers were mucking around with three of them, pretending to vacuum the grass.

'This is getting annoying.' Maddy's white silk headscarf and cats-eye sunglasses gave her an air of dated glamour. 'You think criminal gangs are dumping all this junk here?'

Hilda recalled an article about the deregulation of waste disposal. 'Possibly.'

'I hope it isn't like the toasters,' said Maddy.

'The toasters?' said Hilda, suddenly alert, as if overhearing a secret she assumed was just hers.

'Sorry. I'm making no sense,' said Maddy. 'I keep finding extra toasters around my house. So far, four. I know I didn't buy them. It's a brand I dislike. Very mysterious.'

'Really? That's happened to me, too,' cried Hilda, excited now. 'You don't think some reverse burgling is going on when someone sneaks into your house and gives you stuff?'

Maddy stared at Hilda, mouth slightly open, brow creased, and then shifted her focus to the vacuum cleaners, fisting her hands on her hips. 'Why don't we do something ourselves? I'll fetch my car.' Maddy pointed at the teenagers. 'You ask those kids to load the hoovers in and we'll take them to the dump.' Maddy turned about as sharply as a drill sergeant and strode away.

'You're on,' called Hilda.

At the dump, the women explained the hoovers weren't theirs, just left by fly-tippers, but still ended up being charged £50.

'That's the last time we're good Samaritans,' Maddy said sourly on the way home.

Four days later, ten old washing machines appeared in a neat row by an oak tree in the park. The local news featured the spike in fly-tipping, the presenter, a man in a smart blazer, saying that it was happening in other parts of the city, too. Organised crime was mooted as a possible culprit, and a Labour councillor argued that government cuts meant people couldn't afford to get rid of appliances properly. Hilda didn't buy either theory entirely. Who was discarding so many things at once, and lining them up tidily? No one could explain that.

Whenever Hilda ventured out, she noticed abandoned items—food processors on Mercers Road or music speakers stacked in the Science Fiction section of Holloway library. An unfriendly presence seemed to be pushing into the world, leaving unsettling shapes at the edge of the perceived order of things. Years ago, on holiday in Cornwall, a platoon of yellow plastic ducks—hundreds of them—had washed up on a beach. She'd felt then as she did now—things out-of-place spoke a peculiar language just beyond words.

The neighbourhood packed into the Whittington community hall for a meeting. Mr Khan, Hilda's neighbour, demanded that the council do something, like daily van collections of the rubbish. The council agreed and said they were putting up surveillance cameras, too. Maddy called on people to use their own cars to take stuff to the dump, as long as they could do so for free; Hilda offered to help load items. A woman in pink culottes held up a sign saying, 'Drive out the Evil Machines before they Overtake Us'. The words were ridiculous, but they still sent a shiver down Hilda's spine. *Absurd people see only what they want to,* she told herself, *while other people see absurd things because they are there.*

Back home, she phoned her daughter and confidante. Emily told her it was the same in southeast London. 'These old ovens turned up in the school playground, Mum,' she said. 'My Year 4 kids played a game inside them, but a boy got trapped. We had to call the fire brigade.'

One morning, Hilda bumped into Alviss, who lived above her in the first-floor flat. A short, unassuming man with good taste in music, he had eyes too wise for his twenty-something years. Sadness seemed to hang about him like a dispirited ghost, though she was never sure if she imagined that.

He told her that his work had said not to come in as no computers were working. 'It's as if they've mysteriously all gone on strike.'

'You're saying computers are sentient?'

'Perhaps,' he said with a wry smile.

A few days later, when the early evening sun warmed Hilda's windows, her flat had a power cut. A text informed her that engineers were investigating the problem.

A knock on her door. Alviss stood there in a t-shirt that said, *Go Away, I'm Reading.* 'Has your power cut out, too?'

'Yes. The whole area is affected.'

'I was about to cook but can't now.' Alviss brushed his long fringe off his eyes. 'Do you play chess by any chance?'

'I do. Fancy a game to pass the time?'

'Yes.'

Hilda set up the board on the table.

'You're good,' Alviss said after Hilda took his second bishop. 'I play online. Where did you learn?'

'My dad taught me when I was a child.'

After the match, she chatted with Alviss, finding him easy to talk to. 'Do you have a girlfriend or a boyfriend? I've noticed no-one here with you.'

His narrow shoulders shrugged. 'I'm gay, but I hate dating sites. And I like my own company too much to be a proper partner.'

'I'm rather anti-social, too.'

'Were you ever married? You have photos of that chap and you on the wall.'

Hilda glanced at her favourite, a pre-Emily snapshot of her and a heavily bearded young man outside the City Lights bookstore in San Francisco. Their 'overdose on tie-dye and Bob Dylan era', Walt had later called it. 'That's Walt, the father of my daughter. We were together for twenty years until he died.'

'I'm sorry.'

'It's fine. He passed away two decades ago.'

A ping announced the electricity coming on and Alviss took his leave. 'I've enjoyed hanging out with you,' he said. 'We must play chess again.'

Over the next few weeks, more and more old machines appeared throughout the city. Hilda wondered if the woman with the sign wasn't so absurd after all. The news featured footage of Stamford Bridge football stadium with lorries on the pitch and rusty tractors in Highgate Cemetery. On television, the Mayor told people not to worry because local councils would keep up the removal of the stuff. He agreed it was odd the recently installed surveillance cameras all stopped working in just a few days. Disquiet continued to press upon Hilda until she felt queasy. Reality seemed to have swivelled on its axis, opening a gap between the world she assumed she knew and a more alien one being exposed.

Other people lost interest. Their worry segued to boredom or denial. One day, when Hilda ran into Maddy near a pile of coffee machines on the pavement, Maddy simply said, 'Are you going to the August Fayre on Sunday?'

'But these coffee machines!'

'I'm fed up with worrying about all that. We just need to get on with life.'

Hilda wondered how Maddy could be sick of it all when she'd initially been so concerned. Maybe she'd overdosed on reality. Hilda was unimpressed by the media too, which stopped covering the story. They returned to reporting on celebrity gossip and a politician's affair.

The weather remained hot without respite, and the news occasionally mentioned climate change. Hilda found falling asleep hard, and each morning she stirred uneasily in bed, fending off her nightmares with an outstretched hand, trying to stop them from slipping into her waking. The multi-limbed aliens in her dreams were like a cross between giant vacuum cleaners and levitating octopi. She'd get up and turn on Classic FM to soothe herself, then rub ibuprofen gel into her painful knees.

Power cuts happened more regularly. Electrical devices turned themselves on and off. A two-hour power cut led to another chess session with Alviss.

'Are *you* worried about the machines?' Hilda asked, after checkmating him.

'Yes, but most of my friends want to pretend it's not happening.'

'Why do you imagine that is?'

He pondered. 'Some people have always lived in a privileged bubble. Bad stuff may happen, but never for long, and there's invariably a happy ending. I'm not like them. I don't trust life.'

'Me neither. Any reason?'

Alviss fiddled with the black queen. 'My mum died in a freak accident when I was twelve, so I'm too aware that life's fragile. I often feel like I'm half-expecting an apocalypse.'

'Sorry about your mum.'

'Was it the same for you after your partner died?'

'Even before he passed away, I wasn't complacent. I came from a very poor family.' She twiddled with her bracelet as she collected her thoughts. 'Poverty is a kind of trauma that leaves its mark. But it's given me the ability, too, to face things as they are. Made me less blinkered.'

Alviss nodded. 'I get it. Money and privilege insulate people from reality.' He put the black queen down. 'I've been wondering about the power outages. Perhaps they, at least, are the work of pranksters hacking into appliances.'

'Can they do that?'

'Yes, because of the "internet of things".' Alviss explained that some electronic devices with software exchanged data with others via Wi-Fi. 'They talk to each other.'

'It's weird you mention that, as I'm beginning to think the machines are sentient. Or...' She paused while putting her intuition into words, 'trying to give us a message.'

'A message saying what?'

'I'm not sure. Is there anywhere you could go if it gets worse?'

'No. My parents live in Peterborough, but we're not close. And it's happening there, too.'

Perhaps the entire country will be affected. Or the whole world. Cold needled Hilda's neck.

More and more junk accumulated in her neighbourhood. Only younger children had any enthusiasm for it, squealing as they danced about playing make-believe games. The council vans still picked up what they could, but it wasn't enough. Hilda wrote to *The*

Evening Standard to complain about the lack of broader concern in the problem. Her letter was published, but it changed nothing.

One day, Hilda awoke to no electricity. She dressed quickly. Outside the flat, her breath froze in her throat. Piles of stuff bloomed everywhere: a tower of old tyres ten feet high, cement mixers, a pool of angle-poise lamps. Mr and Mrs Khan, from next door, stood on their doorstep mutely. Hilda waved hello, but they didn't register her. Hilda picked her way down the road and a sense of trepidation rose. Near the end, she met Maddy.

'All these things,' gasped Maddy.

'I thought you just wanted to get on with life.'

'I never imagined this.'

They ventured onto Holloway Road, the main thoroughfare lined by shops, where a traffic jam had formed. Stalled cars, with drivers still in them, were scattered among rusting and abandoned vehicles. The sight of a towering pylon in the middle of the street made Hilda's gut twist. Where had that come from? 'Christ.'

A man leapt out of a car and pelted down the road. Hilda could see nothing to run from. She jumped as an Alsatian dog, as big as a wolf, charged past her, heading after the man.

'What do we do?' croaked Maddy.

'Let's check the official advice.' Hilda scrolled through her phone's newsfeed. The government advised people to return home and stay there while the army dealt with the crisis. She texted her daughter quickly and then explained the situation to Maddy. 'Let's have a cup of tea.'

'How very British, but the electricity's off.'

'I have an emergency gas stove.'

'Clever you.'

Back at the flat, they ran into Alviss. Hilda made three mugs of tea.

'I thought more would be done to deal with it.' Maddy cupped her hands around a steaming mug.

'By whom?' said Alviss.

Maddy received a text. 'It's from my son,' she said,

reading it. 'When the roads are clear, I'll go to his house in Suffolk. The situation isn't so bad there.'

'If the roads are cleared,' said Alviss.

Maddy ignored him. 'What will you two do?'

'This is my home,' said Hilda.

'I'm staying, too,' said Alviss.

A loud bang signalled a crash outside. They all galloped onto the road. Several neighbours stood, mouths agape, including Mr and Mrs Khan. A metal object, about five metres by three metres, had landed. Its thick rusty bars, with gaps between them, curved into a barrel shape that squeaked as it rocked. The leaves of the cherry tree near Hilda's flat shook in the aftermath.

'What the hell?' Alviss's chin tilted upwards. 'Did it fall out of the sky?'

Hilda scratched at her nape. 'It looks like the skeletal torso of a metal dinosaur.'

'I can't cope with this,' said Mrs Khan. She and her husband vanished into their flat.

'I'm going home, too.' Maddy looked as pale as a bone.

'Can I stay with you?' Alviss asked Hilda.

'Of course.'

Hilda spoke briefly with the other neighbours before the two of them went inside. 'One minute,' Alviss said. He disappeared up to his flat, returning with a bottle of wine.

'It's only 11 am,' said Hilda.

'We need a drink.'

'Oh, why not?'

They played chess and drank a glass of wine, which shaved the edge off Hilda's fear.

A beep announced the electricity was back on. A signal on her mobile compelled Hilda to phone her daughter.

'I'm holding up fine, Mum,' said Emily. 'Don't worry.'

After the call, Hilda flicked on Sky News and heard the presenter report that old machines were turning up all over the country. A shot showed fridges lined for miles down the M1. The presenter said the army had been brought in and the Prime Minister was being evacuated to an underground bunker.

'What about the rest of us?' said Alviss.

The television cut out.

They played chess again to distract themselves, and then Hilda made sandwiches to eat. Alviss, who'd drunk three glasses of wine, fell asleep afterwards on the sofa. Hilda retreated to her bedroom to take a nap. She eventually dozed off into a troubled sleep.

Hilda woke abruptly, her heart banging, and ventured into the living room. On the carpet, a vast collection of kettles forced their way into her space. Every hair follicle on her scalp stiffened as she shuffled around them on aching knees. Inert monsters, horror lurking within them, had replaced ordinary objects. 'Go the hell away,' she wanted to shout.

Alviss was asleep on the sofa, with his thumb hooked into his mouth. She wished she could protect him, but it was beyond her. 'Alviss,' she called. 'Wake up.'

His eyes were bloodshot. He let out a yawn, which morphed into a groan. 'What's up?'

'The same, but worse.' Hilda indicated the kettles. 'It's probably only a matter of time before…'

'Before what?'

What did she mean to say? Her lips plucked at words but no words came. Instead, she made herself say, 'Let's check outside.'

It was eerily quiet on the road. Two pylons now loomed into a sky coloured by dusk. A fluid fear seeped into Hilda. She checked her phone. No signal. They retreated inside again and, after moving most of the kettles into the backyard, sat to play another chess game. The diversion offered some relief.

'I need comfort food,' said Alviss.

'How about ice cream? Might as well eat that before it melts.'

They tucked into a mix of vanilla and chocolate flavours, finishing two bowlfuls each.

'Nothing like ice cream in an apocalypse,' Hilda said.

'I prefer my desserts without Ragnarök.'
'Ragnarök?'
'The Norse notion of Armageddon.'

The television burst into life, and Hilda permitted her heart to lilt in hope. On Sky News, a helmeted reporter was in Trafalgar Square. Shrieks sounded off-camera. The reporter pointed at a mountain of televisions, which he estimated to be thirty metres high. 'It's like a monument to... nothing. Or like... we're drowning in our...' His words stopped.

Alviss reached to take Hilda's hand in his.

A loud shriek cut through the quiet outside Hilda's flat. She jumped as if knifed by the sound. Her gaze darted to a framed photo. It showed her cuddling an eight-year-old Emily on Brighton Beach, both in woolly hats. She remembered the chill of the day, her heart bursting with love for her child.

The television went dead.

She tightened her grip on Alviss's hand. How would it happen? Would they be suffocated under freezers? Smothered by pneumatic drills? Starve in a sea of halogen bulbs?

Oh, god.

SNOW ON SNOW

Snow flutters down in her living room, even though the windows are closed. She blinks. The flakes pattern the carpet into white lace and dust the top of her cacti collection. She can't afford to heat the flat, so she puts on a woolly hat and curls up on the sofa, tugging a tartan blanket around her. She gazes at the icy miracle. How remarkable!

When the snow stops before bedtime, she makes hot chocolate and changes into fleece pyjamas. Snuggling under the covers with a hot water bottle, she remembers camping in the garden for a week one December when she was a teenager, sixty years ago; she preferred the quiet, cold tent to the heated rows of her parents. Before she drops off to sleep, the icy tingle on her face tells her more flakes are falling.

She awakes to a flat carpeted in snow, which reaches a few centimetres up the skirting boards and collects footprints when she crunches over it. Nature has adorned the place festively, even if she hasn't bothered to put decorations up. She puts on warm clothes, a woolly hat, mittens, a jacket, and boots. Her bones are chilly, but the magic of this arctic interior lifts her spirit.

Hot porridge warms her. Then, using a pastry brush, she flicks the snow off her cacti collection—the Fairy Castles, Old Ladies, Moons, Stars, Bunny Ears, and Golden Barrels. Her ex-husband said they were like her, prickly but resilient. Worried about what the cold might do to the plants, she wraps strips of hessian around their bases, pricking her finger twice.

With a duster, she wipes the snow off a photo on the wall, revealing her niece and two great nieces in Montreal, Canada; so far away. She doesn't bother wiping the one of her nephew and his family outside Tate Modern, London.

In the afternoon, more snow arrives. Pretty feathers of frost festoon the windows; the mantelpiece and window sills are iced in white. She sticks her tongue out to catch snowflakes, which tickle her with their chill, and then she laughs at how preposterous it all is. Despite her arthritic hands, she clears a pathway from the living room to the kitchen to the toilet, so she can get about safely. That evening, she lays down newspaper sheets to mop up the pools in the kitchen. The chicken roasting in the oven has melted the snow there.

She eats her meal watching a programme about Europe's most famous mummy, Ötzi the Iceman, discovered in the Alps. Preserved by over 5,000 years of freezing temperatures, the leathery remains of Ötzi provoke her to wonder. *Was his life hard? Was he lonely or loved?*

By the next day, her teeth chatter constantly, and deep tiredness is settling into her bones. A trowel is needed to dig her way into the bathroom, and when she pulls down her trousers to go to the toilet, her skin burns cold.

She picks up the landline to call her nephew for help, but then doesn't dial; he is brusque, and she hates being a nuisance. A tear running down her cheek crystallises into ice. She grits her teeth, puts on extra layers, and makes a pot of Earl Grey.

'Hello? Aunt Sara?' A week later, when she doesn't answer the front door, her nephew unlocks it with his spare key. A deep wall of snow greets him.

The firefighters use shovels to get to her. She is frozen solid on the sofa, cradling an iced cactus on her lap.

THE GHOSTS OF CRABS

Dead crabs, lobsters, clams and starfish stretched along the entire beach. Thousands of them packed into a narrow strip, a tangle of oranges and browns.

'Jeez,' I murmured.

It was unusual for ten-year-old Luke to clutch my hand, but he did. 'What's happened, Mummy?'

'I don't know,' I said.

Gulls circled above, their cries raspy. The tide was out and the shoreline was deserted apart from us and a few people in the distance. Pebbles covered the top of the beach, giving way to sand. The creatures were strewn on the pebbled part, so Luke and I trudged along the sand for a brief stretch. The chilly wind licked his dark, curly hair, and sunlight glinted in blades on the grey sea.

'Look! That one's moving.' He ran over and picked a crab up carefully by its back and then carried it to the water's edge. He crouched over it. 'Go on, Mr Crab. Escape.' When it didn't budge, his brow creased.

'Perhaps it's too poorly,' I said.

The old steelworks rose in the distance, a motley line of industrial remnants. Most of it, including the coke ovens and blast furnace, closed almost a decade ago. But here, the past haunted the landscape like a revenant.

'What happens to crabs when they die?' Luke asked.

I was saved from answering by a loud voice behind us.

'I came down to have a nosey.' Fred Black, a fisherman with strong opinions and a weather-worn face, was dressed in a red fleece and wellingtons. He motioned towards the lifeless animals. 'A nightmare, isn't it?'

'It's certainly grim. I assume your catches are affected,' I said.

He nodded sternly. 'I've hardly caught any crabs or lobsters on the boat for weeks. All this started after they began dredging the river last month. That stirred something up in the silt, I reckon. Some leftover poison from the steelmaking days that's killing all this seafood.'

'Why are they dredging the river?' asked Luke.

'To deepen the channel for the new freeport. If you ask me, there's nothing free about 'em. Just a green light for money launderers. That's why our government wants them. A load of criminals, the lot of them.'

I pretended to check my watch to give me an excuse. 'Sorry. We need to get home,' I said. I didn't want Luke dwelling on all this.

'Why did we hurry away?' asked Luke when we were out of earshot.

'I have some work to finish.'

'But I wanted to ask Fred more questions.'

That evening, the crab apocalypse was featured on the local news. The presenter said no one at the Department of Environment, Food and Rural Affairs knew why it had happened. A department official speculated that a 'naturally occurring algae bloom' had caused it.

'Algae blooms have never caused deaths on this scale,' said Matt, my husband. He stopped cutting up onions and stared at the television as the camera panned down the corpses on the beach. 'They aren't even that natural,' he went on. 'The problem is exacerbated by agricultural fertiliser getting into our waters.' He knew this because he worked for a chemical firm.

I turned the television volume down a little. 'Fred Black's theory is that dredging the river has stirred up old toxins in the silt.'

'Really?'

Luke wandered in. His giant African snail covered his outstretched palm, its coiled, tawny shell glistening. 'Goliath will be okay, won't he?' he said.

'It's only sea creatures affected,' said Matt.

'He'll be fine, Lukey Dukes,' I said. 'Put him back.'

I followed Luke as I wanted to collect his dirty laundry. From an early age, he had been heavily into nature, and his bedroom walls held illustrated posters like *Ocean Wildlife* and *Mammals of the World*. After placing Goliath in his glass tank, Luke sat on the floor to play with the Lego fox he had recently built. I stayed for a bit, chatting with him.

That night, a voice woke me. Without disturbing Matt, I crept out onto the landing. A cool wind eddying up the stairs made me shiver. I hurried down, tensing as I saw the back door open. Then I heard Luke speaking outside.

When I flicked the patio light on, he twirled around. He was barefoot, his skinny ankles sticking out from the bottom of his favourite Scooby Doo pyjamas. 'Mummy!'

'Who are you talking to?' I peered into the garden.

'No one.'

'But you were.'

'I had a dream about the dead crabs, and then I woke up and came down…' His gaze darted about. 'Oh.'

'What?'

'The light must have scared them away.'

'Scared who?'

'The ghosts. The crabs and lobsters. They're made of shadows.'

He wasn't a boy given to tall stories. It crossed my mind that a few real crabs might have got in—our garden backed onto a large field, behind which stretched the sea. But I could see nothing.

'Did your dream frighten you?'

'You don't believe me, do you?'

'I know you don't make up stories, Lukey. But come on. Bed.'

The next morning, while Matt buttoned up his ironed white shirt, I mentioned Luke's antics.

'Don't worry. He's just over-imaginative.' Matt picked up his tie.

'But it was out of the ordinary.'

He shrugged. 'Let's keep him away from the beach until they've cleared the creatures up and he'll be fine.' He put the tie on. Matt always looked immaculate.

The following Saturday, when Luke and I visited the beach again, the dead animals were gone. But the atmosphere was disquieting. Clusters of grey clouds menaced the horizon, and dirty white foam crested the waves as they came in, slapping onto the sand like a frothy mesh.

The sea held Luke's attention, leaving him quiet and distracted. 'Was Fred right that there's old poison out there?'

'We shouldn't jump to conclusions.' I stroked his hair. 'But don't worry. Grown-ups will sort out the problem.'

His expression said he didn't believe me.

'Come on. Let's go to the farm shop and get some nice things for lunch,' I said.

That night, I woke abruptly in the early hours, shivering as I recalled a dream of shadowy crabs crawling across the floor. Unable to fall asleep again, I slipped downstairs.

Luke was in the garden once more, so I crept to the door. The moon cast an eerie glow. He was crouching on the grass with his back to me, saying, 'I'm sorry. There are so many of you and no one…'

I stepped onto the patio, trying to be quiet, but knocked my foot against a ceramic pot.

Luke spun around. 'Mummy!'

'What are you doing?'

He glanced about. 'Oh! They've gone again.'

'You mean the crab ghosts?'

'You don't believe me, do you?'

'I believe you saw something.'

'No, you don't.' He ran inside and upstairs, shutting his bedroom door. I followed him and by the time I opened the door, he was under the duvet. 'It's not just me who sees them,' he said. 'Curtis does too.' That was his best friend, who liked to take his cues from Luke.

'Do the ghosts scare you?' I asked.

'They make me sad.'

'Go back to sleep now, poppet.'

On waking the next morning, I filled Matt in, admitting I had concerns about Luke.

'Try not to worry. It's just him being a kid.' He got out of bed and drew the curtains. Warm sunlight flooded the room.

I rose too. 'I'm not sure it's that straightforward. Let's at least keep him away from the news.'

Matt let out a breath. 'If you say so.' He slipped on his grey fleece dressing gown. 'Did I tell you Conrad Sheply has been commissioned to do an independent survey on the crab deaths? The fishermen are paying for it.'

'Oh?' Conrad was a consultant in marine pollution, whom Matt had known for years.

From then on, Luke spent more time in his bedroom and didn't join us to watch Dr Who or Blue Planet in the evenings. At dinner, he ate his meal in silence, and if we asked how his day was, he'd shrug and say, 'Okay.'

I went into Luke's bedroom one evening and his radio was on quietly, tuned to the local station with the most coverage of the crab story. So much for keeping him away from the news. He was at his desk, creating a picture.

'What are you drawing?'

He showed me a picture of four crabs on a yellow sandy beach. Two were only sketched, two had been shaded in black.

'Still worried about the crabs, poppet?'

With a shrug, he resumed his drawing.

It occurred to me that it might be wiser to include him in any conversation about the dead animals. I talked to Matt later, and he said, 'Good idea. We can't mollycoddle him forever.'

While we were all eating toast in the kitchen the next morning, the local television channel reported that the Department of Environment, Food and Rural Affairs had confirmed the algae bloom theory. They dismissed the notion that a chemical from the steel-working days was responsible.

Matt turned the volume down on the remote. 'I don't trust DEFRA these days. Let's wait and see what Conrad Sheply says.'

'I agree,' I said.

'I hope we get the truth,' said Luke. 'The crab ghosts can go home then and find peace.'

'I get you are concerned about the crabs,' said Matt. 'But stop this talk of ghosts. It's silly.'

Luke wolfed down his last bite of toast and stood up. 'I need to feed Goliath.' He disappeared into his bedroom.

'Do you have to be so direct?' I said.

'I don't believe in lying to him.' Matt crossed his arms.

I bit down on my lower lip as my gaze settled on a pre-Luke photo of Matt and me on the wall. On the beach, the steelworks behind us, arm in loving arm; Matt wearing his lilac beanie hat and baggy Radiohead t-shirt that I hadn't seen in years.

The following week, Conrad Sheply appeared on television, saying that pyridine, a chemical toxin that had been dumped into the estuary for more than a century and settled in the sediment, was being stirred up by recent dredging. The surly spokeswoman from DEFRA argued the chemical occurred naturally in crabs, but Conrad pointed out that the dead crabs had over fifty times more of it than was normal. 'That's the reason for the deaths,' he said.

The woman shook her head irritably, claiming his findings were based on too small a sample. 'And Mr Sheply's findings align too conveniently with the beliefs of the fishermen who funded the research.'

That comment drew fury from the fishermen. Fred Black appeared on the local radio the next morning. 'If you ask me, it's a government coverup. We're protesting outside the town hall from 4 PM. Come and join us.'

When I picked up Luke from school, he was keen to go to the protest.

'I'm not sure that's a good idea,' I said, worrying he would repeat his night antics in the garden.

'I have to do something for the crabs. Please, Mummy. Please.'

I gave in, deciding to trust my son more. A good-sized crowd turned up, and Fred welcomed us warmly. Luke asked to hold Fred's sign, *Stop the Dredging, Stop the Crab Deaths*. A newspaper reporter took pictures.

The following day, Luke and the sign were featured in the local paper. I cut out his picture and pinned it on the fridge. Luke offered a thumbs up.

Luke and I became regulars at the protests, which took place weekly near the town hall and received plenty of media coverage. I was surprised by how much buzz being involved in an environmental cause gave me. I hadn't felt this committed to anything for years, and Luke was also fired up. He made a sign on cardboard to take, *Save The Crabs*, and he started bringing home environmental books from the local library too, like *101 Ways For Kids to be Eco Heroes*.

In response to the protests, the DEFRA spokeswoman conceded on television that 'further testing suggests Conrad Sheply is probably right. The river dredging will halt while an independent panel examines the evidence.'

Luke jumped around the living room, whooping, 'Yes! Yes!'

I smiled and clapped my hands, happy that Luke had got me involved.

On Saturday, a couple of Luke's friends came over for the afternoon. The boys spent the time in the garden building a den and I was pleased to hear them all giggling.

At 1 AM, after using the toilet, I opened Luke's door to check on him. Too much silence drew me in. His head was under the covers. I put my hand on his bed. The lump underneath felt too soft. Pulling back the duvet revealed a pile of clothes. I peered into the garden from the window. No one there. My stomach dropped. I searched the house, then woke Matt up and told him Luke was missing.

He jumped out of bed. 'Let's phone the police.'

An idea flew to me. 'Let's check the beach first.'

We dressed quickly, armed ourselves with torches, clambered over the back fence, and sprinted across the field. A full, ashen moon loomed in the sky, haloed by a pale glow, and the cold air made my eyes stream. My heart thumped so loudly it was audible in my ears.

We crunched over the pebbles at the top of the beach, with me shouting, 'Luke!' The expanse of landscape swallowed up my cries.

Matt spotted a torch flashing way down on the

shoreline. We hurried over. Thank god it was him, facing the water. He spun around as we approached, the wind ruffling his hair.

'What the hell are you doing out here?' Matt's face was tight with anger.

'We were worried,' I cried.

'I'm holding a funeral for the crabs,' said Luke.

'How dare you run off in the middle of the night on your own,' Matt barked. 'You silly boy.'

He held a posy of sweet peas he must have picked earlier from our garden. 'I wanted to say a proper goodbye so the crab ghosts can rest in peace,' said Luke. 'I wanted to tell them I'm sorry that stupid humans poisoned them.'

I had been angry with him too, but this sweet gesture melted my heart. 'Have you finished?'

'Not quite,' said Luke.

'Finish up and then we'll go,' I said.

Matt scowled at me, but I met his gaze. 'Let him,' I said.

Matt held up his palms. 'Okay.'

Luke offered a few farewell words for the animals, then threw his posy into the sea. The languid waves rolling in sang a hushed hymn.

We returned home in silence, Luke in front, Matt and I a few metres behind. Matt took my hand in his. As we neared the house, he said quietly, 'You think that's the end of the ghosts saga?'

I nodded.

'Well, I hope he'll be okay,' he said. 'I mean, with the crappy, polluted world he's growing up in.'

'I'm proud of him. He's been empathetic and brave, our own little Greta Thunberg. It's like his imagination has dealt with the environmental disaster more honestly than we have.'

Luke must have heard because he stopped and waited for us to catch up. When he tilted his chin up towards me, a quiet smile gathered at the corners of his mouth. Then he took my hand and led us back home.

THE WOMAN WITH BIRDS IN HER HAIR

A finch darted from Avecita's hair, landing on one of the wooden perches in her kitchen, and sat there twittering. Birds twitched on her hair too, which was piled up behind her head—a gravity-defying bun, as long and wide as a fox's tail—and kept in place by grips and clips, on which her feathered friends balanced.

'Calm down, you lot. You know, I'll be back by lunchtime,' she said.

Avecita finished boxing up the cakes and desserts, then quickly tidied the kitchen and fed the chickens in the coop next to the vegetable beds outside. A couple of three-year-old apple trees were in bloom. Seeing the pink blossom brought a slight lump to her throat—she'd planted them in memory of her parents, killed in a car accident—and the birds on her hair started a sad warble too. 'Let's try to be happy today, eh,' she said. 'The sun's out, it's spring.'

She'd lived all her twenty-five years in the white cottage at the edge of the village. 'See you later,' she called as she locked the yellow front door. Of the dozen birds—finches, bluetits and sparrows—that shared her life, only three were brave enough to accompany her into the village, perched atop her bun.

Cow parsley and columbine peppered the grass verge of the lane that meandered towards the village's heart. The sun warmed Avecita's cheeks; fat white clouds drifted across a cerulean sky. The three birds trilled merrily as she walked, only falling silent when she turned into St Helen's Street. 'Don't fret,' she told them. They suddenly chittered in fright.

'Look! It's the hairy bird freak.' Sam Spader stood across the road with a few friends. The lanky teenager, who had a floppy fringe and a mean mouth, lived in one of the posh houses nearby.

Avecita's chest tightened in fear. The school holidays must have started; Sam spent term time at boarding school. She hated it when he reappeared, and herself too, a grown woman afraid of a schoolboy. She'd known too many Sams at school herself, boys—and girls—who'd made life miserable, 'the girl with birds in her hair' an easy target. After all these years, it was happening again; it had done so since Sam turned fourteen.

Her heart rate spiked as he swaggered across the street and encouraged the lads to follow. When he wasn't around, the other teenagers ignored her.

'I've got a question. How often do you wash that ridiculous mop? Once a year?' He sniggered, and his friends did likewise.

She stood motionless and mute, her words choked by anxiety.

Sam crossed his arms. 'Well? I haven't got all day.'

'Sam!' Mrs Appleby was approaching, her body hunched over a silver-topped walking cane, her pearl necklace glinting in the sunlight. She glanced at Avecita, then focused on the boy. 'You're home from school then, young man.'

'Yes, it's Easter holidays. How are you keeping Mrs Appleby?' Sam's switch from boy beast to youthful charmer was instant.

'Very well.' The woman's eyes smiled. 'Going away anywhere nice this time?'

'No. Father has far too much work on his plate.'

'Never mind. Now be a good boy and leave Avecita be.'

'Just messing around. You know me, I'm always the joker.' He flashed a smile and then beckoned to his friends. 'Come on. Race you to the beach.' They sprinted after him.

'Boys will be boys,' said Mrs Appleby. 'Good day to you, Avecita.'

Boys will be boys? Avecita thought in disbelief. *Really?* She'd watched the lad and the old woman talk, as if a spectator in someone else's dream. Mrs Appleby was better than many villagers who simply ignored Sam's bullying. The idea of him here for the next few weeks wrapped dark ribbons round Avecita's heart and her birds jittered with concern, too.

She was relieved to reach High Street, where a number of pedestrians were out and about. A hand-written sign in the window of the Co-op advertised Avecita's wares: cakes and desserts made to order.

The outdoor market was at the end of High Street, near the church. Three mornings a week, Avecita had a stall here. Even if *she* wasn't popular in the village, her cakes were. A few locals refused to buy from her, muttering about hygiene and feathers, but Avecita's animals were well trained and her kitchen was immaculate.

As she set up the stall, her birds balanced atop the canopy rather than on her bun. A couple of early customers—tourists probably—gawped at Avecita's hair. She looked away, focusing on her cakes. The lemon drizzle was a perfect mix of sharp and sweet; the Victoria sponges moist and light; and the chocolate brownies rich and chewy.

She sold six meringues to Johnny Bigdon, a kind man who'd played in the local orchestra with her dad. 'What's in these, Avecita? They're so good.'

'Just sugar and eggs from my chickens.'

'No secret ingredient, then?' he said with a gentle grin.

She shook her head, aware of the rumours that something extra was in her bakes, a magic ingredient that made them special. In truth, she merely followed her recipes faithfully, having always loved cooking.

'Johnny. We need to get off.' His wife shot Avecita a sharp look.

Avecita knew the other rumours too, that certain men from the village visited her at night. *If only*. Avecita recalled the only lover she'd ever had, a thin, serious civil servant from a nearby town, whom she'd met via a newspaper dating column. After a series of happy months together, he started complaining about her birds. 'You have to shut the things outside. I'm not having them share the bedroom with us any longer,' he snapped. He walked out on her when she refused that.

Later that morning, a stout woman, who looked too funky for the village, stopped at the stall. She wore a turquoise jacket over black harem pants and a turquoise scarf wrapped around her curly greying hair; multiple bracelets jangled from her wrists. The woman's face cracked into a smile, crow's feet gathering in the corners of her intelligent eyes. 'These look very nice cakes.'

'Thanks.'

'And what accomplished hair you have.'

A surprise. People normally avoided mentioning it. She smiled bashfully. 'Are you on holiday?'

'No, I've just moved into the Old Rectory up the hill. Someone told me there were perfect cakes at the market. I have a sweet tooth, as you can see.' She patted her bulging tummy.

Avecita had heard of a woman buying the big house at the top of the village, a successful author, apparently, who wrote under a pseudonym, although she wasn't sure what kind of books. 'So you're the writer.'

'Among other things, yes. My name's Clara.'

'Avecita.'

'Pretty name.' She studied the cakes. 'I'll take a lemon drizzle and four carrot cupcakes.'

As Avecita took the money, she was shocked to see a long, snake-like form dart out from inside the woman's jacket. *What on earth?* Clara caught hold of it and absent-mindedly twirled its end around in her hand. It was a strawberry-blonde tail, like a lion's, with a bushy tip.

Avecita had heard of people with tails, but had seen them only in books and newspapers, never in this remote village or even in the nearest town. Weren't they rare? 'That's a very nice tail.'

'Yes, I think so myself.' Clara lifted one side of her jacket to reveal a thin plastic hoop, about 10cm in diameter, sewn into the lining. 'Get back in there now, naughty,' she said to the tail, which obligingly looped itself round the hoop and hung there. 'It sometimes has a mind of its own,' she told Avecita.

While Avecita had affection for her birds and her hair, she never spoke openly about them to anyone.

Two days later, as Avecita was walking to the market,

she spotted Sam Spader again with a couple of lads. Her veins turned chilly.

'Hey, hairy bird weirdo,' he called. 'Ever get bird shit in your barnet?' He stopped in front of her, hands fisted on his hips.

'Don't talk to her like that,' barked a voice.

Avecita's head twisted to see Clara striding towards them, irritation written on her face.

Sam jerked his thumb at himself. 'Tourists don't tell *me* what to do.'

'I'm not a tourist,' said Clara.

'Oh?' A frown flickered across Sam's face. 'You're... not that woman who writes books, are you?'

'Doesn't matter who I am. What matters is that you cannot speak to this lady or anyone else in this manner. Please apologise.'

Sam stared at her, open-mouthed, and his friends studied their feet, faces flushing pink. Then he composed himself quickly and forced a smile. 'I was only kidding around. Avecita here is used to my teasing, aren't you?'

Avecita refused to grace that with an answer.

'It might be a joke to you, but it isn't to the person on the receiving end,' said Clara. 'Apologise. Now.'

A lump came into Avecita's throat. In the years since her parents had died, no one had come to her defence like this.

'Well, we're waiting.' Clara raised her brows.

He set his jaw rigidly before muttering, 'Sorry.' Then he took off with his friends.

'Are you okay?' Clara asked Avecita.

'Fine. It's... nothing, really.'

'It isn't nothing. Why did you let him talk to you like that?'

'I... I....'

Clara softened. 'Let's hope he won't do it again.'

On her way home later, Avecita hummed as she strode along, and her birds joined in with an uplifting tune.

However, back at her cottage, a few of her birds were on the buddleia bush by the gate, sharply flicking their tails and clacking their beaks. The front door was splattered with eggs and several vegetable beds were torn up. *Vandals!* An intuition flickered: Sam Spade was responsible. Avecita was sure of it.

When the local police officer arrived, she explained what had happened, including her suspicions.

PC Burman was a burly man with a sour expression. 'You know who Sam's father is, don't you, young lady? Got to be careful going around making claims like that. He might sue.'

She knew he was a bigwig lawyer in the city up the coast, who had a reputation for giving large donations to politicians and throwing his weight about on local issues. 'But it was Sam. It had to be.'

'There's no proof.'

'Couldn't you take fingerprints?'

'Not for petty vandalism. As you're a bit isolated here, I'd recommend you put up a security camera to deter vandals in future.' Before leaving, he advised, 'Be careful about repeating your allegations regarding Sam to anyone, okay, young lady.'

Left on her own, she felt shaky, anxiety clinging to her thoughts. The birds wouldn't settle either, leaping from her hair to a perch, then rapidly back again. That night, she couldn't sleep and eventually got up at 3 AM to make herself custard. Then she stared blankly in the kitchen mirror, at her bloodshot eyes and thick brown wavy hair falling to her waist. Every night, she took out all of her clips and grips and brushed her locks out, just as her mum had done when she was a child. How she wished her parents were still there, her dad's elegant flute colouring the evenings, her mum bustling hither and thither, a vigorous hub of energy.

The following day, on her way to work, Avecita was tight with tension. Fortunately, Sam didn't appear. A workman came to her cottage that afternoon to fit stronger locks on the doors and a security camera. Then her shoulders could relax.

On Friday, a loud knock on the door caused Avecita to jump. *Who's that?*

Clara was there. 'Your cake was delicious. I'm having some friends over next weekend and wonder if you might make a birthday cake for my friend and a selection of puddings.'

'Of course. Come in, please?'

The woman joined Avecita at the kitchen table for a cup of tea. Clara took off her jacket and sat down. Her tail wound itself several times around the bar on the back of her chair, dangling its end like a tassel. She described the cake she wanted—shaped like a parrot and with bright red icing. 'Can you do that?'

'Of course,' said Avecita. 'Any story behind it?'

'Why not come for tea and cake on the day and see for yourself?'

Nobody ever invited Avecita to parties. 'You're sure?'

'Very.' Clara looked around. 'What a charming kitchen.'

The small room was painted azure and primrose yellow, with a dresser on one side, and over the walls were nailed little blue perches on which the birds could rest. 'Thanks.'

'Do the birds help you bake?'

Avecita checked the woman's eyes to ascertain if she was being facetious, then smiled and shook her head.

'I find my tail incredibly useful for things like…' The tail uncurled, reached out, and wrapped itself around the salt cellar, picking it up. 'See?' The tail then replaced the item. 'But it makes wearing clothes tricky. I need holes in my pants, trousers and skirts so it can poke through.'

'You like having a tail, then?'

'I adore it, but it can get in the way, and some strangers feel entitled to try and touch it. Honestly!' Clara rolled her eyes.

The manner in which Clara talked openly and proudly about her tail made an impression on Avecita, who usually felt shame in public about her hair and birds.

'What do you like best about your birds?' asked Clara.

Avecita thought for a moment. 'How they always know what I'm feeling.'

Clara left eventually, saying she would pick up the cake and puddings the day before the birthday tea.

The following weekend, Avecita arrived at the Old Rectory for the party in a freshly ironed lilac dress. Wisteria swarmed up the front of the Georgian house. As she rang the doorbell, the three birds in her hair chirped nervously.

Clara, in a lime-green trouser suit, opened the door. 'Come in.'

The large living room had an open fireplace and sofas; original watercolours dotted the walls. A table displayed sandwiches, puddings, and the birthday cake. Five guests strolled through a doorway, and Clara introduced Avecita to them. 'This is the genius behind the cake.'

'It looks fabulous, darling.' A slender man, in a silky red cardigan and with a macaw sitting on his head, clapped his hands.

'Ed's the birthday boy,' said Clara.

'Ed's the birthday toy,' said the parrot. It was scarlet, with azure and emerald feathers in its wings.

Ed sashayed over, hips swinging side to side, and held out an elegant hand. 'Lovely to meet you.'

For once, it was excitement, not fear, that stopped Avecita from speaking. She grinned at the macaw and shook his hand.

'You have the most delightful hair,' Ed told Avecita.

'I love your parrot,' said Avecita.

The bird ruffled its wings. 'I love your carrot,' it said.

Avecita had never met such people. The other five greeted her warmly, too. Two men, a similar age to Clara, had little goat's horns on their heads, and the sets sparkled with silver tinsel decoration. A younger woman, introduced as Clara's niece, had a tail like her aunt's. A cloud of tiny lilac butterflies fluttered around the final guest, a handsome man with eyes the colour of forget-me-nots.

Clara served the cake. 'To the birthday boy.' She held up her teacup as a toast.

'To the birthday boy,' everyone exclaimed.

'And to all you beautiful freaks,' said Ed.
'To all of us freaks.' Avecita flushed with enthusiasm.
'To all of us beaks,' said the parrot.
After cake, Clara poured them all a glass of wine and suggested they play board games.

Avecita's finches deserted her for the horned men. The birds had never taken to anyone else before.

Avecita beat Clara twice at chess.

'We must play more often,' said Clara. 'You can teach me strategies.'

'I learned from my dad,' said Avecita.

'I learned from my sad,' said the parrot.

Time flashed by as fast as a swift, and Avecita was reluctant to leave. On the walk home, her heart bubbled with joy, and a newfound confidence settled into her. It was as if she'd stumbled on a long-lost family or a secret club to which she'd always belonged.

At the start of her lane, Avecita froze in fear.

'Hey, hairy bird freak.' Sam Spader was alone. 'What's it like to be such a weirdo?'

She took a deep breath and forced the words out: 'There's... nothing wrong with... being me.'

'There's... nothing wrong with... being me,' he mimicked.

Her mind flew to the afternoon with her new friends. Something small and folded inside her began to swell. It opened, growing stronger and bolder, until she was wrapped in it. The words that spilled from her lips took even her by surprise: 'Leave me alone, Sam Spader. You're a bully. And if you ever vandalise my cottage again, the security camera will record it and I'll have you arrested.'

His mouth dropped open as she strode past him.

As she headed home, her birds trilled out a wayward song.

Vanity Vines

'I simply cannot deal with this today,' exclaimed Helena. She was sitting in her dressing room in front of an enormous mirror. Under the light from the chandelier, she examined a vine sprouting from her scalp.

'Let me take a look,' I said.

Her TransPlant was *Senecio rowleyanus* or 'string of beads'. It was six months old, long enough for the plant to be well established on her head, and its stems trailed pea-like leaves. The many bobbly vines framed her face on either side and were chopped across her brow into a shaggy, pea-green fringe.

Up close, I noticed a few vines had yellowed at the ends. I frowned. Not something I was used to seeing as a TransPlant stylist. 'You are taking the PlantVit supplement?'

'Of course, Rosie.'

'And you use the feed spray daily?'

'Do something, for Christ's sake,' she snapped, ignoring me. 'This afternoon's audition is for Calvin Klein.'

'I'll trim the bits off and try you on another supplement,' I said. My love of being a TransPlant stylist thankfully made dealing with her more bearable. The best-paid models were high maintenance.

Using miniature secateurs, I spruced up her hair. Then I spritzed it with BioSpray for shine, which carried a light jasmine scent. 'There you go.'

Admiring her reflection in the mirror, Helena said, 'Mm. Dreamy.'

Outside, on the front steps, I glanced back at the glass-fronted luxury apartment block where she lived. Since the film *Eve* came out, featuring Sadie Sink as a kick-ass temptress in Eden with a TransPlant down to her thighs, I'd become a regular visitor to such places. I'd even been mentioned in *Vogue*. Fancy that! Me, who owned a tiny semi and bought her clothes at H&M, in a chic magazine.

May, my next client, owned a plush flat with a balcony on the riverfront. She had a startled appearance, as if she didn't quite trust the world was real. Her three-month-old TransPlant was *Hoya linearis,* great for a hair substitute because of its slender cylindrical leaves which hung gracefully. The thick, jade-green waves draping down either side of May's pretty face suited her.

'It's grown lopsided this time,' she said. 'See?'

The vines on the right came to below her shoulder, about two inches longer than those on the left. Again, this wasn't something I'd come across before, and concern flitted through my mind. 'Hmm. You might be using the feed spray unequally on either side. But don't you worry! I'll tidy it.'

I used tiny secateurs to prune. I could see where the dense vines emerged from her scalp. The initial procedure removed all natural hair, seeding a myriad of vines instead in the follicles beneath the skin. 'The plant looks in good condition,' I said.

'Well, it cost me enough, hun.'

'True.' It was £50,000 to have a TransPlant. I fantasised about getting one, but no way could I afford that.

I tidied up the last bits. 'You're still okay with the sleep helmet?'

'Fine.' May used a spherical helmet at night. It helped protect the plant from damage. More hardcore clients like Helena slept upright in a foam-lined container.

'Hopefully, you'll have flowers before too long.'

She smiled. 'You know I've gained 80,000 followers on Instagram since I had it done?' May earned her money as an influencer.

'Really? Nice outfit, by the way.'

'Thanks.' May smoothed a hand down her skin-tight lilac sundress. 'I just can't eat in this—or breathe.' She had a smoker's throaty laugh, at odds with her sweet persona.

I gave her hair a final spritz while she studied herself in the mirror. I knew I was a good stylist. My previous jobs as a hairdresser and a shop florist made me right for the work, and I'd been one of the first to complete the training course.

I had four more client visits after May, two of whom had the same problem as Helena.

When I got home, Kai, my husband, was in the kitchen, cooking curry by the smell of things. Radio 2 was playing in the background. 'Hey,' he said.

I kissed him on the cheek, then squeezed past to pet Haru, our cat, by the door.

'How was your day?' Kai asked.

I told him about the unexpected hair issues.

'I thought TransPlant was above all mortal plant problems,' he said, raising his bushy brows cynically.

'The clients can't be following their instructions properly.'

'Let's hope you're right.'

I spotted the brochure for the parks and gardens of Tokyo on the kitchen counter and felt my spirits lift. 'I paid the deposit for our holiday today,' I said.

'Can't wait.'

Kai longed to visit Japan, where his paternal grandparents were from, but we'd never been able to afford it on our combined salaries as postman and shop florist. In the last year, my income had tripled thanks to my TransPlant stylist job, and it was to be my special treat for his thirtieth birthday. As my gaze rested on the perfect wisteria on the brochure cover, Helena and May's hair came back to mind. An unease settled in my gut. I dismissed the feeling, telling myself I was worrying about nothing.

***

A week later, when I visited May, her TransPlant was not just longer on one side but thicker, too; noticeably asymmetric.

'Looks weird, doesn't it? I haven't posted content on Instagram for a day,' she said. 'I'm a wonky head.'

Nervous laughter pecked from her. 'You have to laugh, don't you?'

'I'll do a trim. Have you rung the Chevairte helpline? Chevairte was the first and best TransPlant company, and I recommended it to clients. Dr Alan Magnolin worked there, the genius who'd first developed the TransPlant procedure.

'I couldn't get through. Chloe O told me in a DM she has the same problem.'

That evening, I looked up #TransPlant on Instagram and found nothing odd. I saw Chloe O's post about taking a 'social media detox' break. She had the succulent *Senecio Herreianus* as her TransPlant, with its oval-shaped green leaves on vibrant purple stems. She posted pictures with her edgy boyfriend, who had a feathery-leafed Boston Fern on top with bald sides.

I closed down my phone and started my evening beauty routine using the Estee Lauder products I treated myself to these days: cleanser, serum, eye cream, night moisturiser, neck gel, and face oil. I loved pampering myself in this way; the expensive products made my skin feel healthy and soft.

Kai appeared in his pyjamas and gave me his sceptical, 'How much does that lot cost?' look.

'I pay for them.'

'I know.' He held his palms up in a conciliatory gesture

For the next few days, there were no TransPlant incidents, easing my concerns. But then Helena phoned, sounding distressed. I drove over later, hoping it was just model melodrama.

She answered the door in sunglasses, her breath heavy with whiskey. 'A bloody nightmare.'

'Let's see.' I shepherded her into the dressing room. She sat, crossing and uncrossing her legs. An empty vodka bottle lay on the floor.

A weight settled over my shoulders. Her TransPlant was worse than I expected. Several vines were spotted with tiny brown pustules and four had yellowed five centimetres at the bottom, like they were dying.

'The verdict?' she asked.

'Um... not sure.' It was unwise to tell Helena I hadn't seen this on a TransPlant before.

She whipped her sunglasses off, revealing bloodshot eyes. 'You've got no idea?'

'It looks like blight or rust, something common in normal plants.'

'Ugh!' Her palm flew to her brow. 'Aren't TransPlants GM, or whatever it's called?'

'They're genetically altered to be resistant to plant diseases. I'll chop off the rusty bits, but it won't be perfect for a few days.' I didn't voice the concern that the rust might spread.

'But I have a Maybelline audition tomorrow.'

'I'd cancel it.'

She let out a breath and stared at her phone while I pruned.

'God! It's not just me. Char Wiggins has posted a yellowing vine.' She held up her mobile to show me. 'I did a fashion shoot with her last week. Did she infect me?'

'It's likely someone there infected the others.' I wondered, too, if the disease had jumped species from a normal plant. Observing Helena's perfect model body tainted by blight conjured a momentary smirk on my lips, but I suppressed it, reminding myself how much she paid me.

The next week, an article appeared online, calling it 'hair blight'. The journalist blamed those who'd opted to have TransPlants: *For a time, TransPlants seemed problem-free, but interfering with nature like this is never without risk. Some people have more money than sense.* This from a magazine that had regularly featured celebrities with plant hair since the trend began a year ago. What hypocrites!

May was the next client to make me go cold with worry. Some of her bead-shaped leaves had become discoloured, and a few had developed grey mould. It looked like downy mildew, another fungal infection of plants, and close up there was a slight whiff of mildew.

'What on earth am I going to do?' she said.

'Chevairte will come up with a solution.' I tried to sound more confident than I was. I cut off all the damaged foliage, bagging it up in plastic to burn later, and told her to snip off and burn any bits that showed signs of the disease. Because I thought she could handle the truth, I explained that mildew might be hard to contain.

'Really?' She fiddled with her necklace.

That afternoon, another client messaged, saying: *I'm getting horrible white spots on my TransPlant. I regret taking your advice to have it done.* I tried three times to get through to the Chevairte helpline but kept being put on hold.

To distract myself from the worry, I went shopping for holiday clothes for Kai and me. I imagined us strolling in Kyoto through heavenly cherry groves.

The fungus problems spread, and within a month, social media was full of suggested remedies: oregano antifungal sprays; herbal tinctures; chemical fungicides. Some claimed these stopped their hair disease; others shared pictures of withering TransPlants. The comments below the posts varied from '*poor you*' to '*ha, you no longer rock—you rot!*'

Several clients cancelled appointments, making me anxious about them and my finances. Having not heard from May, I checked her Instagram and saw she hadn't posted for two weeks. Guilt stabbed me—I was the one who'd originally recommended her a TransPlant. I messaged to ask how she was but with no reply. I tugged at my blouse's neckline, wondering whether to message again.

Chevairte and other TransPlant companies declined media interviews and issued only generic press releases. They were 'investigating the issue'. My emails to them went unanswered. Dr Alan Magnolin, once hailed as a genius, vanished abroad; no one knew where.

The next time I visited Helena at her flat, my gut dropped. Coppery and brown hues speckled half her head as if it were autumn. She stank of booze and slightly of dead leaves, too.

'I haven't slept in ages. I've lost thousands through work I've cancelled.' Her jaw clenched.

I told her it was best to shear off the entire TransPlant, back to its roots, starting from scratch. 'Okay?'

'I've got no bloody choice, have I?'

When I was done, her bald skull was dotted with hewn vines. She dashed out of the dressing room. Sobs could be heard in the bedroom. Later that evening, her personal assistant texted me to say he'd checked her into The Priory Clinic and so was cancelling her next appointment with me.

'I feel bad,' I told Kai.

'Helena is the sort to have a nervous breakdown over putting on two kilos,' he said.

'May has ghosted me. That makes me feel worse.'

'But this isn't your fault.'

'I advised May to have the TransPlant.' I pointed at myself.

His brow creased. 'Did it really never occur to you that something like this might happen?'

'No. I trusted Chevairte,' I snapped. 'Plus, we can't live on your salary alone, can we?'

'Don't start.' Kai's mouth flattened to a line.

In the bedroom, I began my Estee Lauder beauty care regime with a leaden heart. I enjoyed having much more money and didn't want to go back to using cheap products that irritated my skin or bickering with Kai over bills. Still, I felt guilty about taking my frustrations out on him. Before we went to bed, I apologised.

On Instagram that week, Chloe O posted that she'd tried bleaching her TransPlant with hydrogen peroxide to stop the mildew, but that had withered it more. Photos showed her Medusa-like, with grey vines snaking from her head. Chewing my lip, I watched a live Instagram event in which her boyfriend chopped off her TransPlant. Tears slid down her cheeks. Finally, they threw the plant into a wood-burning stove.

Hashtag #burntheblight took off, and social media was filled with videos of sheared TransPlants being tossed into bonfires. Angry bald celebrities announced they intended to sue the Transplant companies. Wig sales spiked.

One client emailed to call me a 'stupid bitch'; another to say she was angry and considering suing me: *I can't get any model jobs with this damn rot on my head.* Tension filled me, and I showed the email to Kai.

'She should be suing the TransPlant company,' he said. 'I read an article yesterday that a class action lawsuit is being launched by several people against Chevairte. You could reply suggesting she joins in with that?'

'Or I can ignore her. I can't be legally responsible. I'm just a stylist.' I was more shaken up than my words let on, though.

Over the next few months, the TransPlant horror story unfolded further. Online articles said that some, though not all, people with the rotting vines were developing health issues—migraines, fatigue, skin rashes. A rare Chevairte press statement suggested that these were 'caused by anxiety' but hinted that they would offer to remove implanted vine roots from individuals for free if any legal claim against them was dropped.

It took me ages to get to sleep each night. I'd lie stroking Haru, who purred in the dark. My dreams were intense: I'd be doing a client's hair when they'd suddenly become a zombie, eyes the white of poison ivy, mouth smeared with blood. 'Stupid bitch,' they'd growl. I'd wake abruptly, heart banging.

They're right, I realised at 2AM one morning. *I've been a fool.* Kai had guessed that messing with nature in this way might have unintended consequences. Why hadn't I? I lay surrounded by the night, shame crushing me.

My work dried up completely, so I took a job at a local hairdresser. I liked the soft touch of real hair and wasn't facing fraught clients, but losing a big chunk of income stung heavily.

One evening, I summoned the courage to tell Kai I couldn't afford our visit to Japan.

'Damn. I was so looking forward to that.' His shoulders hunched.

I hated letting him down like this. 'I'm so sorry.'

The following day, the electricity bill arrived, and we both avoided opening it.

I bumped into May one Tuesday in the Tesco's car park. I hardly recognised her at first because of the dark wig and how ill she looked—dark bags underscored her eyes and on her previously flawless skin were large patches of spots. Having not heard from her in months, I blushed in embarrassment. 'How are you?'

Frowning, she said she was unwell, still waiting on her deTransPlant procedure, and she was part of the court case against Chevairte.

'I noticed your Instagram has gone,' I said. 'I'm so sorry about what happened.'

'I keep asking myself why I had it done.'

'We were all naïve.'

'You can say that again.' She looked about to cry.

An awkward silence hung and I didn't know what more to say, so I made a weak excuse and got into my car. Guilt stalked me all the way home.

One night, I spotted Helena in a Lynx advert on television. The latest hair craze, animal fur transplants, had replaced her TransPlant. Dog and cat pelts were the 'in thing' and her mane of Pyrenean mountain dog looked truly strokable.

'Does it suit her?' I asked Kai.

'She looks like a weirdly glamorous werewolf.'

'Do you think the animals are used ethically?'

'I don't know.' He grinned slyly. 'But I was thinking how often dogs such as that get fleas.'

'Or ticks.' I smirked, too.

The Carp Whisperer

Takiki's hands sweated on the steering wheel, her mouth was claggy. She spread out her fingers to let the breeze play. Only in moments of privacy did she allow herself this freedom. The childhood taunt 'Takiki's a freakiky', could still make her feel shame about the webbing stretching from finger to finger.

The car behind blared its horn; she snapped her fingers together as though caught in a crime. 'Alright! Alright!' she muttered. Manoeuvring around a pot-hole, she crawled onto the ring road, where the traffic was bumper to bumper. If she was late, she'd be fired and then what? She'd dry up like all the others who couldn't afford the water truck. About to work herself into a panic, she saw a billboard at the side of the road and managed a smile. Grey-haired folk waved from the doorsteps of quaint cottages, like they'd found a slice of heaven. Behind them, stretching up to the corner of the poster, were patchwork fields of fruit and vegetables with a river snaking through them. The legend, written in white across the clean blue sky, read: *eDen Island, D-class Retirement Homes.*

Auntie Letitia had signed up for a place at eDen as soon as Takiki had found her job in the city over a year ago. Six months later she was gone. I'll write again tonight, Takiki thought. But she knew the letter, and all the ones she'd written over the months, couldn't be sent until the postal service was up and running. God knows when that would be. When the rains fell again, perhaps, when the world started working the way it should.

At Lot 17, she scanned the tarmac for a space. There! As she pulled in, a strange light rippled along her car. She lifted her head to the lorry directly opposite her. Through its open door, she could see rows of glass tanks filled with clean blue water. It was as if she'd fallen into a dream, a time from the past when such things had been possible.

She looked around, expecting A-Quantrol Guards with machine guns protecting the precious cargo. When she saw none, only D-workers walking with bowed heads to the checkpoint, she leapt out of her car and onto the burning tarmac before she could stop herself. She lifted her face to the water. It was so clean, so blue, except… there! A flash of colour… Another. Gold and red and silver. What the hell was that?

'You took your time.'

She jumped. The owner of the voice appeared from inside the lorry, a Thor baton dangling from his belt. In his hand, he held a clipboard.

She took her step back. 'I'm sorry. I didn't mean to—'

'Well, you're here now.' When he came closer, she knew, from his deeply tanned skin and broad nose, that he wasn't an A-qua, nor a B-class, or even a C. He was a D-class worker just like her. But still a man with a Thor baton, a man who had caught her staring at the water.

He tucked the clipboard under his arm and she spied the picture at the top: a thin-faced young woman like her, with long braids and black skin. 'You kept me waiting for half an hour.' He twisted his head to read the name on the board. 'Lola Burken.'

She was about to tell him she wasn't who he thought she was, when a big fish, golden-red, twitched its tail against the side of a tank. The man moved closer, and she had to wrench her head from the sight of the fish to listen. 'This was a stupid place to pick you up,' he said, 'too many low-lifes. Mate of mine was knifed for one of these buggers not so long ago. *And* I had to switch the aircon to save on gas. If any of the koi are dead, you'll be going straight back.'

Koi? Was that what they were? She'd thought they were extinct. In her village, the lakes and ponds had given their water to the sky and in the hollows, black mud cracked, turned hard as brick. Now she saw that in some other place—eDen maybe?—there was water enough for a fish not to be eaten but cared for in swells.

'Come on up,' said the man, and tossed her an ID pass.

Without even glancing at it, she slung it around her neck. He pulled the door shut behind them and the only light came from the tanks. She didn't think to be afraid of the man in the enclosed space, saw only the water and the fish with their sunset colours: red, orange, gold and silver. The webs of her fingers pulsed oddly.

The man plunged his hand into a tank and reached for a thermometer lying on the bottom. Not looking at her, he said, 'Don't just stand there. Do the rest. Gotta be 37.5C'

The world tilted a little as she lifted a tank flap. With the very tips of her fingers, she touched the water and found it cool and soft, like no water she'd ever known. She wanted to plunge in, let it rush over her face, work its way into her braids, lift each follicle. She snaked her hand towards the thermometer.

And then, then, the fish came.

It was as long as her forearm, fat and sleek. She twisted her hand, and it settled its belly in her palm. Out of the carp's mouth came a grape-sized bubble. She was so close she saw herself reflected in the sheen: her black face, the wide eyes. Another bubble rose and this time Takiki shone gold. The final reflection showed only the fish inside the bubble, swishing its tail.

'You done there, missy?' said the man. 'Don't you worry your head about the rest of them. Good old Jack, heh, doing your work for you.' He walked out of the lorry and jumped to the ground. 'Act sharp, girl. We're already late, thanks to you.'

Without another word, Takiki joined him in the front of the cab. As they drove away, they passed the D-workers waiting at the checkpoint. That was where she should be. Not here in a lorry-load of fish. She studied the man out of the corner of her eye, working up the courage to tell him to stop and drop her off, when she noticed a tattoo peeking out from under his shirt cuff. She gripped the door handle. The tattoo was of a Fire Serpent. Only D-gangsters had those. What kind of strings had he pulled to get a job like this?

The man shot her a glance. 'You look about to jump,'

he said. 'I know it's tough when you first get back, but you need to keep your shit together, focus on the endgame. Am I right or am I right?'

She forced herself to nod, afraid to ask what he was talking about: admit that she had no right to be there. She'd heard stories of the revenge this type of man would take: beatings and stabbings over the slightest misdemeanour.

They stopped at the checkpoint to the inner city, a place Takiki had never been before, never would have been allowed. An A-Quantrol Guard walked towards them, a semi-automatic in his hands. As he reached over to accept the man's papers through the open window, he saw Takiki and raised his gun. Takiki shrank back in her seat.

'Hold it,' said the man. He stabbed at a piece of paper. 'Legit 529, special circumstances. We got here a Carp Whisperer.'

The guard scrutinised the paper, then stared up at Takiki before waving them through.

A Carp Whisperer? Hadn't she heard of that before? She delved into her memory and emerged on a night so hot that even the stars and the moon seemed to sweat. Sleep was impossible, and she had called out for a story. With a pile of sewing on her knee, Auntie Letitia had told her a tale of a people who talked with carp.

'Why would they want to?'

'Carp are fishy clever, they listen and watch. A person who can talk to them will learn things. Not only that.. ' She put down her sewing. 'Carp Whisperers can shape-shift too.'

Takiki hitched up in bed. 'What's that?'

'Turn from person to fish and back again. But it has to be a good reason, not just because they fancy it. They must first learn something so important that they have to swim back to their people to tell it.' She leaned over and stroked Takiki's hair. 'You, with those beautiful hands, maybe you have the fish magic. Sleep now.'

When she'd left, Takiki thought of the fish magic for a long while, then decided Aunt Letitia was trying to make her feel less like a freak. This story was nothing but an old wives' tale, something to whittle away the night, and she'd packed it away.

She lifted her head to shake the memory and saw, for the first time, the trees which lined the road. They were sun-scorched and twisted but majestic, alive. She'd never seen so many together. She swivelled in her seat to take in the white marble buildings, the window boxes bursting with reds and yellows.

'We play the game right,' said the man with a grin. 'We'll be living in one of those fancy apartments soon as dammit. I got my eye on one down Perch Avenue. Two more years and then I'm owed.'

Was that true? Could this job lead to that? A D-class man in the A-qua sanctum? The man was a fantasist, a dreamer, to think such a thing was possible. The best people like them could hope for was an extra litre or two of rations, and the promise of eDen Island when they retired.

A slip road took them to some steel gates manned by four A-Quantrol Guards with semi-automatics and sunglasses. The man waved his papers, and they were let through into a tunnel. The lorry shuddered as the engine died. 'Let's get to it.'

As she clambered down, the air smelled cool, of water. She'd thought that she'd be even more scared upon reaching their destination, but there was a fluttering in her gut, an excitement. She ran over to the back of the lorry and watched as the man stepped up and unhooked a trolley from the side. 'Your friend first,' he said. She got in beside him and together they unclipped the clasps that held the tank to the wall and lifted it onto the trolley. The carp swished its panic. 'Calm it down, for God's sake,' said the man. 'I had one die of fright last month.'

She stared at him.

'Speak to it. That's your job, isn't it?'

She wanted to say that she didn't have the words, that this had been a terrible case of mistaken identity, but as the carp splashed, a rhythmic throb started in her gut. She clamped her hand on her belly as it coursed up through her throat and bubbled out of her mouth, a sing-song chant, deep and soft.

'That's it,' said the man when the carp settled and nosed itself towards the music. She stared at it, a bubble of joy in her chest. 'Keep going,' he said.

She would, she could. Crouched over the tank as it was pushed, she sang to it… no, with it: its gills pumped tiny spheres of air, words which were not quite words, yet Takiki found she understood. *All I am, you are too.*

Oh, how well it sang, how clever it was.

We are water, we are life.

The song died as the man stopped to key in numbers on a huge metal gate. Takiki put her hand on the glass, wanting the koi to continue. Sing to me.

The fish made no response, even as it was pushed into the sun and the tarmac gave way to a slick marble path beneath Takiki's feet. *Please sing.* Nothing. Just a twitch of its tail. Takiki felt its silence as a strange sensation of cool air just behind her ears. Keeping her eyes on the fish, she lifted her hands and explored a welt, soft at the edges, as though a cut had healed.

'Quite something, isn't it?' said the man.

She dropped her hands, afraid. But the man wasn't looking at her, but at the view.

She stood straight. 'Oh!'

They were standing in a wide open space in what must be the heart of the city. It was as big as her village and filled with ornamental ponds, small lakes and fountains, some linked by narrow, man-made streams. Pale stone walkways, lined by tubs of pink and blue flowers, crisscrossed the space and the hot sun danced in diamonds on the water. She spread out her hands. 'It's… it's…' she trailed off, unable to find the words.

'Yeah, it is.' He laughed. 'That apartment I've got my eye on is behind that building.' He pointed into the distance where a fringe of white balconies faced a lake. 'Imagine waking up every day and smelling this damn beauty of a place.'

'Where are all the people?'

He paused. 'It's like... they don't know how lucky they are. Hardly any of them use it 'cept at weekends.'

'All this water. Is there...' She furrowed her brow, trying to remember the word, 'a spring here?'

'Nah, pipes bring it from the old wells north of the city.'

She took a step back and he must've seen what she was thinking because his mouth went tight. 'Keep your trap shut about this place outside work,' he said.

She stared at him.

'I mean it, girl. The A-quas get even a whiff of you blabbing and you're in serious shit.' He ran a thumbnail across his throat as if slitting it. 'Two more years, I've got, two more. I don't need no trouble.'

She took a deep breath, settling her racing pulse. 'Okay, I get it.'

He searched her eyes and gave a curt nod. 'You wait with the fish. I'll go and sort out the paperwork.'

She watched him walk down a path and vanish through some glass doors. By her side, the carp slapped the water with its tail, and, as though its song was in her head, she heard, *It's yours, it's yours.*

The song hummed in her head and belly, thrummed her fingers, behind her ears. She moved without wanting to and found herself at the edge of the ornamental pond. Her legs obeyed the song, and she squatted, tilting her head to where the water rippled with a soft current. Her chest constricted, and for a moment, the song stopped.

Just like the man had said, there was a dark wide hole in the wall where fronds waved as water streamed gently through. She pictured the pipe snaking under the white marble houses and guarded city wall, under the ring road, across the scrublands, and then further out to the arid hills and the villages. Her village.

The song began again, high and piercing. *It's yours.* She stared at the pond glittering with sunlight and tried not to listen. But the song was inside her and her throat was dry as parched tarmac.

It belongs to you, to your people.

Her webs twitched and the strange cuts behind her ears throbbed as she knelt and pressed her face into the water. She gulped cool water, and it slicked down her dry throat.

Take care!

From nowhere, the man was by her side; before she could leap away, her hand was wrenched up her back 'What the hell are you playing at?' His calloused hand burned on her wrist as he twisted her round to look at him. 'They'll send you back there. Only this time you'll be on the receiving end.'

Her eyes were fixed on the Thor Baton: one zap she'd be unconscious, two dead.

'Don't you think I get thirsty too?' he spat. 'But I'm not such a fool. I'm never going back to eDen.'

Takiki's world narrowed to a tunnel, the man at one end and her at the other. 'eDen?'

He shook his head. 'Don't give me that. You sanitised the olds too.' A vein pulsed on his neck. 'We had no choice, did we? Natural resources have to be conserved.'

As Aunt Letitia waved her hanky from the window of the mini-bus to eDen Island, she'd been going to her death? Not just her, but most of the olds from the villages. Why? Because they weren't even worth their three litres a day? Better to use their rations to fill a pond, have another cherub spewing water.

What bastards!

She tried to wriggle free, but the man was too strong. Beside her, the carp flashed, slapping its tail. *Free yourself.* The man held the baton out to her neck and his thumb shook a little over the button. 'Stop struggling,' he commanded.

As she closed her eyes, the song rang within her. *Be brave. Be free.* She jerked her wrist and opened her fingers, spreading the webs wide. As he saw the strange pale flesh, his grip faltered.

There was no thought as she ran: only thick muscles under her glistening skin, only the smell of the water and the song humming in her veins. *We are water. We are life.* With one last glance at the man standing, Thor-baton in hand, she hurled herself over the side wall of the pond.

In the air she was skin and bone, limbs and lungs; as the water met her, she felt herself shrink, become dense, packed and powerful. Her legs jerked and fused; her flesh became sinew and scales. Gills opened, a tail swished, a sleek body slid. She twisted her spine, flicked her fins, and in front of her was the blank gaping hole of the pipe. She was a fleeting streak of red-gold heading upstream back to her village. She would sing out the news to her people. *We are water. We are life. Resist. Be free.*

EXISTENTIAL SHRUG

'I'll get whatever you want for when you return,' I told Sofie. 'Anything.'

A sly look flashed in her gorgeous green eyes like she was planning a secret underwear party for a priest. 'How about the lyrics of a Cosmic Flunk song written on a cloud?'

'Okay.' That was our favourite band.

'To be precise, the chorus of "Existential Shrug".'

'Sure you want *that*?'

'It's so *you*, Rook.'

I was seeing her off at the port. She was going home to see her folks. As soon as I'd waved goodbye, I wanted the holidays to be over. I'd never felt so besotted by a girlfriend, although it weighed on my mind, too, that she was only twenty-two while I was a year off thirty.

Back at my ground-floor flat, I distracted myself by researching commercial cloud advertisers. At short notice, the above-board companies like CumulusAds would write on clouds in particular locations: £300 per word. For £240 per word, you could have any cloud, but it might be floating over Bognor Regis or Glasgow. No good. I had to get some money together and find someone to do it on the cheap.

In my backyard, I walked past all the hutches. The doggits I bred—hybrids with a rabbit's head on a long-haired Dachshund's body—pressed their noses to the wire mesh, tails wagging. Selling on Animix wouldn't cut it, not after all the taxes and fees. Luckily, I also dabbled in the bootleg market. Which doggits to sell? Jimi and Bob, probably—I named my animals after musicians. Jimi and Bob's white coats made them worth more. That colouring was popular with rich folk because it was unusual. 'Sorry guys,' I said, stroking their noses.

It sucked to be spending the festive season alone—my sister had fled to Portugal ten months ago when the state of emergency was declared—but now I at least had a mission. On Christmas morning, I headed down to Opa Garage, opposite a Tesco with a row of inflatable Father Christmas decorations in front. No longer a garage because of the fuel ban, it was good for bootleg shenanigans. A 'closed' sign hung on the door, but to one side, a kiosk sold snacks, hot drinks, shots of Upper-T, and Zizzy pills. Sure enough, a motley gang of regulars were at the wooden tables, in woolly hats and coats, playing chess. Ed the Head, a bloke with a lot of contacts, was engrossed in a game with Dave the Burp, a sour-faced grump who could belch for England.

I ordered a coffobomb from the kiosk and then wandered over to their table. Ed took Dave's bishop. It looked like a checkmate in four, and I hoped that would put Ed in a good mood. I was a chess master, with an ECF rating of 2360. It was my passion from when I was a teenager, an antidote to the frustrations in my life back then. My nickname came from my reputation at my local club for forcing checkmates with my rooks. I'd met Sofie there fifteen months ago.

After winning, Ed looked up at me, his cold blue eyes staring out from beneath his trapper hat. 'Want something, Rook?'

I asked about cloud writing. I wasn't sure he was listening because his gaze drifted back to the chessboard, where he reset the pieces. 'What's in it for me?' he said.

'I'll give you a game.' The blokes here liked me playing them—they could boast about how long they'd held out.

'You never play unless you're certain to win, do you?' Ed gestured for me to sit.

After I checkmated Ed in a mere twenty moves, he said, 'Your best bet is Elsbeth Wupland, but she won't be around until after Christmas.' He jotted down her phone number and address for me on a piece of paper. 'Don't ask her to write anything tacky, okay?'

'What do you mean?'

'She's fussy. Likes to think of herself as a creative type, not a glorified advertiser. Doesn't do soppy or cliches or commercial stuff.'

'What's the point of creating anything these days?'

Ed made a noise like a snorting pug. 'Tell her I sent you, right?'

A loud bang shook the air. All our heads jerked around. Dark smoke swirled from where the inflatable Father Christmases opposite had been.

Ed stood to take a better look. 'Probably the anti-Christmas League.'

The ACL had originally used graffiti to object to all the money spent on Christmas displays when so many people were struggling. Recently, they'd graduated to blowing up decorations, including a fluorescent snowman on the High Street. I shrugged and suggested another game to Ed. He sat down and we played one more before the military police arrived at Tescos. Then I skedaddled. Those pigs might arrest you just for being there.

On Christmas day, I watched trashy films. *Bad Santa* came on after lunch, which made me think of Dad. No doubt he would stink of whiskey by this time and be banging on about the government or pawing his latest squeeze. I didn't remember Mum well; I was only ten when she died. I changed channels to watch *The Grinch* instead, one of Sofie's favourites. Then I called her to tell her how much I missed her.

'Miss you, too,' she said.

After we'd chatted for a bit, she asked, 'How's the cloud writing coming along?'

'All taken care of.'

She paused. 'Do you know someone hurled a burning oil drum through the window of Barclays Bank in Green Square?'

'So what?'

'Please be careful. Nonchalance won't protect you from stuff like that.'

'I'm fine. Have you played your dad at chess yet?'

'He used the Evans gambit, and I didn't even get to an

endgame.' She sounded gutted. Sofie was competitive, but her father was a chess grandmaster.

'Want to talk through the match with me?'

We spent a while working out where she made mistakes. About half of our relationship was analysing chess games together—when she came over at weekends, we'd lie for hours in bed doing just that.

'At least Dad took me for lunch at Kontrast afterwards,' she said.

That was a posh restaurant; Sofie had expensive tastes. Hearing about her life in Norway made me worry I didn't have enough to offer her. I envied her closeness with her folks, too. Kontrast probably wouldn't let my dad through the door.

On December 27th, I rang Elsbeth Wupland and her answerphone told me she'd be back at work on the 29th. *Damn*. Another two days. I killed time by going to Green Square, where protests were taking place over Christmas. Sure enough, a mob had gathered. Signs held up demanded rent regulation, an end to the ban on unions, fair elections, and free Zizzy pills. I stayed for a bit, seeing if I could find anyone selling Zizzy pills on the sly, but I legged it when four vans of military police turned up. I'm not hardcore about riots.

Elsbeth Wupland worked out of an abandoned warehouse complex at the edge of the city, part of an old industrial estate from the time of democracy. I parked my e-car and pulled a Taser out of my satchel. Places like this attracted dodgy sorts. People rarely mess with me since I'm well over six feet and in good shape, yet my satchel still carries an arsenal: a Taser, pepper spray, and a hunting knife. Not that I'd ever used the knife.

I found a sign on a door that told me to take the lift inside up to the office. The slow lift creaked and finally opened onto a flat rooftop under an unseasonably blue sky with no clouds. Staring at me from a chair was a wiry woman with a purple beanie hat and too many facial piercings. Her green work overalls, worn over a fleece jumper, were spotted with flecks of coloured paint. She quickly bent to pick up a baseball bat. To her left were a bunch of paint cans and a tan boxer dog on a leash, which leapt up. 'And you are?' Elsbeth said.

'Rook. Ed the Head gave me your address.'

'Put that thing away.'

I replaced the Taser in my satchel and walked over, the wind ruffling my hair. She chucked the baseball bat down.

The dog growled. 'Bilbo. Stop that and come here,' she said. It slunk to her side, and she petted it.

'Why are you on the roof?' I asked.

She made a vague gesture towards the sky. 'Sit down.'

Both chairs were bolted to the rooftop. She continued petting the animal, which eased my concerns about possibly selling Jimi and Bob to her. I explained I wanted a lyric on a cloud.

'I don't do clichés and stupid pop songs, you know.'

I handed her a piece of paper with the lyrics.

She read it. 'You sure you want *this*?'

'Yup.'

'Roughly speaking, where do you want the cloud to be?'

'Over the south side of the city on January 2nd.'

She nodded. 'Any colour?'

'Not red.' Sofie had a thing about red and refused to eat food that colour. It made things tricky as I put ketchup on everything.

'Well, I can do that for two thousand four hundred quid.'

'What about bootleg equivalent?' I took a photo of Jimi and Bob out of my satchel and handed it over. 'Two white doggit pups?'

She studied the picture, then eyed me suspiciously. 'Where would you get hold of these?'

'I breed them.' I gave her a business card.

'I'll take one doggit as a down payment, the other on the day that the job's finished. Okay?'

'I need to know you'll sell them on to someone who'll take proper care of them.'

'No problem.'

'You promise?'

'Sure. I might keep one myself. These white ones look gorgeous.'

'How do you do cloud writing, by the way?'

'I go up in the air harnessed to a Pedodrone, with one of those.' She indicated what looked like a large paint sprayer. 'A cool bit of tech. It sprays not only pigment but also this chemical called Cumul-Z, which condenses water droplets within a cloud into lines that form the letters.'

I didn't ask how she avoided the military police airdrones. Probably she bribed the pigs, which wasn't uncommon.

At home, I prepared Bob for transport, stroking him before putting him in a travel crate. A pang of sadness hit; I got too attached to my animals. I returned to the warehouse and presented him to Elsbeth along with a bag of doggit food, plant protein pellets. Her dog sniffed at the crate, wagging its tail. Bob's tail whipped back and forth in response.

'He's adorable,' she said. 'I'm going to keep him.'

That evening, I phoned Sofie to tell her the cloud was being done now.

'Oh?' She seemed distracted. 'I read that someone set fire to that Christmas tree in Shelley Place yesterday.'

'Really?' I didn't follow the news. Sofie was always fretting over something in the papers, but I was inured to it. The bombs, riots, protests, floods, wildfires, heatwaves, shortages—all background noise to me. Ever since my early teenage years, I'd felt impervious to most things, and what good did worrying like Sofie do?

'There were twenty peaceful protesters arrested there yesterday, too,' she said.

'So what?'

'Why do you never care about anything besides your own little world? Your friends are all the same.'

'I care about you.'

'It's always chaos over there,' she said.

I scratched my jeans with a thumbnail. 'I can't wait to show you the cloud. I used Bob and Jimi to pay for it.'

'Is Adele still there?' That was Sofie's favourite pup.

'Of course.'

'Sorry, Rook, but Mum has just come in pointing at her watch. I have to go. We're off to the theatre.'

'Sure. Love you.'

'You, too. Take care.'

Unsettled by the chat, I hurried out to pet the doggits. Adele's coat was so soft. 'Sofie will be back soon. You love her too, don't you?' I said and her little Dachshund tail went ten to the dozen.

A day later, I rang Elsbeth Wupland to check how things were going. 'Bob has hit it off with Bilbo,' she said.

'Good, but I meant with the cloud.'

'That'll be done. Don't worry.'

On the day it was due, I took Jimi over to Elsbeth. Bob was ecstatic to see him.

'You'll love the cloud,' she said. 'I finished it earlier. The wind speed is pretty fast today, but Spring Hill should be an excellent spot to view it.'

I drove to the port, imagining Sofie's beautiful face lighting up when she saw the cloud. But when I got there, a text arrived. She hadn't boarded the boat as she promised last night. She hadn't even left her place. I scrolled, trying to understand what I was reading. *I'm so sorry, Rook. I care about you a lot, but the politics really gets to me. I'm not sure we'd work out in the long term, anyway.*

So she'd figured out there were better things to be had elsewhere. Better boyfriends, too. I parked up and walked around the south side of the city for hours, hands thrust deep into my pockets. The barest thought of Sofie would conjure the image of her and sadness would wash over me like wastewater along a gutter. Then hot anger at her would blaze and I'd kick an old bottle on the pavement, sending it skittering, or mutter 'the bitch'. I'd sold Bob and Jimi to pay for that stupid bloody cloud.

Having all these emotions was so weird!

I eventually found myself on Spring Hill. A couple holding hands looked upwards. I followed the woman's pointing finger. Christ. *My* cloud. Elsbeth had done it beautifully, in looping blue handwriting on a large cumulus. Tears smeared my eyes as I read:

To be or not to be—
a question for a mug.
Me? I'm all about
the existential shrug.

The Art of Rubbish

Biscuit found the first one, on the beach on a sunny morning. After snuffling around, he barked madly—odd behaviour for a placid Labrador. 'Sit down. Shush,' I said. He sat there, wagging his tail and whining. 'What's up with you?'

My eyes were drawn to the plastic debris, and while I realised it was arranged to spell out words, it took a minute to work out what they said:

SoRT iT ouT!

The letters—some capitals, some lower case—were up to half a metre tall; half-buried in the sand and with parts weighted down by pebbles, they couldn't blow away. The first letter, S, was made from torn pieces of soft plastic pinned under pebbles; the second, O, from a pink plastic ring, the kind dogs play with; and the third, R, from a round lid and plastic bottles.

Underneath was an unhappy smiley face drawn in the sand—a perfect circle, about a metre in diameter—with tiny shells filling in for the eyes and mouth.

What did it mean? It looked too skilful for kids messing about. The beach, a mix of sand and pebbles, swept along for about a mile, but as usual at 8.15 a.m. on a weekday, no one else was around. I took a shot for posterity on my phone before picking up the debris and putting it in the canvas bag I always carried. I was part of a group who collected the rubbish here, ever since an official cleaning of the beach had seen over a thousand pieces of plastic rubbish picked up every 100m, much of it tiny bits, but larger stuff like bottles too. A great deal washed up because of the location and currents.

I turned for home, a brisk twenty-minute walk away, and soon I'd forgotten about the words. It didn't occur to me that more would appear. A busy day loomed—I worked from home, building websites for clients, after which there were the usual chores, including shopping for my housebound mum. Then, in the early evening, I sat down to dinner with my daughter.

Frannie was a determined eighteen-year-old into art and environmental causes; all youth and zeal, even if I didn't approve of her silver nose ring.

'How was college?' I asked.

'There are fifty-one trillion, apparently.' Frannie was often caught up in her own mind.

'I'm not entirely with you.'

She fixed her thoughtful eyes on me. 'It's how many pieces of plastic are in the ocean. We read an article about it today in Geography. What with doing the plastic picker stuff, I thought you might like to know.'

'I pick up what I can. Fifty-one trillion is a little beyond me,' I joked.

'You know what I mean, Mrs Ostrich.'

Her nickname didn't ruffle me. Although I admired Frannie's passion for the student climate protests, my main advocacy was for an easier life. Work and the caring I did for Frannie and Mum were all I could handle. I'd only volunteered to pick up litter because I could do it on my dog walk.

'Tell me more about your day,' I said.

'Well, in art we looked at mermaid beach art and listened to a podcast by that Hellier woman.'

'Oh?' I'd met the writer, Juliet Hellier. She was a local author who had hired me a few years back to produce a website for her books, including two on mermaid beach art published a decade ago. 'What did she say?'

'She talked about the beach art mermaids make. Pre-Raphaelite in style and with scenes of them combing their hair or communing with seals.'

'Not your sort of thing, is it?'

'No way,' Frannie said. 'But it's cool how they always create their pictures in situ out of organic materials: sand, seaweed, shells, stones. Technically, it's ace. Just doesn't do anything for me.'

'It did when you were at primary school.' At that age,

Frannie forever pestered me to take her out on the tourist boats to the more remote coasts. There, you sometimes saw mermaid art on the beach or even, on a rare day, glimpsed the mermaids themselves from a distance.

'I was just a kid.' She was indignant. 'Their art isn't exactly Banksy, is it?'

My mind harked back to the words on the sand. Perhaps whoever did it found inspiration in mermaid art. It wouldn't have been the mermaids themselves, as they never came to our beach—it was too popular with people—and Juliet's book, which I'd once read, made clear that their style was, as Frannie said, Pre-Raphaelite.

'Is Juliet one of those mermaid fansters?'

Frannie's question disrupted my thoughts. 'I don't think so.' That group went out and did rituals in honour of the mermaids, leaving offerings such as candles on beaches; definitely not *my* scene. Before I met Juliet, I assumed she was into that kind of thing, but afterwards, I had doubts. She didn't look the part—she wore smart floaty dresses, not hippy tunics and leggings—and her curt manner made her hard to fathom. Like an Escher painting, intriguing, but you couldn't quite make out how they worked.

Later, I listened to Juliet's podcast myself, then checked my emails. One plastic picker suggested that our group move beyond litter picking into campaigning work. My heart sank, and I went to bed thinking up excuses.

The following week, Biscuit and I found another word written in plastic on the beach:

ReVoLTiNG!

Beneath it, an angry face stared up, a metre wide and sculpted cleverly in sand, pebbles and strips of plastic; its narrowed eyes sat above a down-turned mouth, the irises and pupils filled in with grey and black pebbles. Was some artist or even an environmental group behind it? I took a shot on my phone and left it be, intending to pick up the plastic bits tomorrow. Biscuit kept sniffing at the thing and barking, though. In the end, I had to drag him away.

I drove down Ferry Road, where I noticed Juliet Hellier herself walking on the roadside, and stopped to offer her a lift.

'Ta, Beth,' she said as she got in. Under her long mane of brown hair, streaked with grey, shone green eyes that scrutinised you. Like her house, which I'd visited once, she smelled a little aromatic, of freshly brewed coffee and cinnamon. She turned and made a fuss of Biscuit in the back seat. 'Lovely dog.'

'He's called Biscuit.'

Her handsome face cracked into a smile. 'Does he like biscuits, then?'

'Too much.' I drove off. 'My daughter, Frannie, listened to a podcast from you in her art class at college and enjoyed it.'

'Oh?' Juliet shrugged.

I'd noticed before that praise made her awkward. 'Did you see that word written in plastic down on the beach?'

'You mean "revolting"? Yes. Nicely done.'

'There was "Sort it Out" a few days ago, too.'

'Really?'

'Yes. Any idea who's behind it?'

'I'm not aware of any local artists doing that kind of thing.'

'The mermaids?' I said as a joke.

'No. Way too punk for them. My money's on talented teenagers or art school students.'

I wondered if Frannie and her friends were responsible. Her artistic talent made it a possibility, and I had to admit I'd be proud if it was her.

'Do mermaids even learn how to write?' I asked.

'A few *are* literate, but not loads of them.'

Juliet's cottage had a stone sculpture of a mermaid in the front garden. Before getting out of the car, she said, 'You've got my text number, Beth. If you come across any more words on the beach, message me.'

'Okay.' Her enigmatic smile perplexed me. Was she

herself responsible? After all, she was a painter as well as a writer.

'By the way, I'm part of a new local group linked to a national anti-plastic coalition. You wouldn't be interested in designing a website for us?'

'Paid work?'

'No. Voluntary, but a good cause.'

'Sorry. I'm a single mum who also cares for my mum. Too much on my plate, anyway.'

'Shame.'

Over the weekend, I felt disappointed to find no new words. Far more people walked on the beach then, so perhaps that put off whoever it was. However, the following Thursday, I punched the air with excitement. A whole phrase in plastic:

Do SoMEThING ABoUT iT!

Underneath, sculpted out of sand, shells, and plastic, sat a large, Medusa-type head. Snake-ish coils of hair radiated from the face; wide staring eyes lay above a mouth open to reveal sharp teeth. It was artistically done, but perturbing, to be honest. I was unsure what it meant.

That evening, I mentioned the words to Frannie, showing her the photos on my phone.

Her eyes widened. 'Cool. I've seen nothing about this on Instagram.'

'There's nothing on the local Facebook page, either. It isn't you or your friends, is it?'

'No.'

Four days later, my heart bubbled with excitement when I came across yet another:

SOd THe PLaSTiC!

This time, the sand and plastic picture beneath was a hand making a V sign.

Biscuit scampered off to bark at something fifty metres down the beach. Maybe a seal, by the size and shape; we occasionally saw them here. I broke into a run, worrying that a seal versus dog stand-off might turn nasty. As I got close, I halted, my mouth dropping open in surprise. In all my years, I'd never seen one of these on this beach.

She spoke in a Northumbrian accent: 'Put that dog on a leash.' She glared at Biscuit, who stood a couple of metres away, whining.

I grabbed hold of him, told him to sit, and, after putting him on the leash, focused on the mermaid. Her scaled tail, a streak of silvery-brown shot through with oily colours, was speckled with tiny barnacles and a good two metres long. She was sturdily built and her large breasts sagged from a broad chest. Her ginger hair, clotted with seaweed strands, tumbled in snake-like clumps to her waist; no fine Pre-Raphaelite locks. Her hands were frilled with webs. I blinked.

'What are you staring at?' Her eyes radiated contempt.

'Not every day you see a mermaid.'

'We try to steer well clear of you lot, too.' She flicked her tail irritably.

An idea flew to me and I pointed down the beach. 'Was it you?'

'Pardon?'

'The messages written in plastic in the sand.'

'Yes, it was.'

'But that isn't your normal style of art.'

'Says who?'

'The book I read.'

'A few of us make different kinds, you know, though you lot appear obsessed by the stupid, fanciful stuff.'

'I've seen no pictures of mermaid beach art like that before.'

'So? Doesn't mean it doesn't exist.'

'Well, I find it intriguing. I prefer it to the fey stuff.'

'Really?' Her sarcastic tone suggested she didn't believe me. 'In truth, there aren't many of us making this kind. Maybe a few more recently.'

'Why's that?'

'Duh! All the plastic.' She reached out a hand and,

grimacing, scratched at what looked like a small laceration on her tail.

'Are you okay?' I asked.

'I cut myself on something here last night. It got infected—that's why I'm stranded. The infection has weakened me a little.'

From where I stood, I saw the cut contained pus. 'Anything I can do to help?'

She ignored me. 'I never used to feel weak like this before all the plastic appeared. It's messing with our bodies.'

'I hate plastic waste, too. See this?' I indicated the bag on my shoulder. 'I pick up rubbish every day here.'

'You want a medal?'

Was there anything to say that wouldn't annoy her? 'Can I help at all?' I repeated.

She pointed to the shoreline, about twenty-five metres away. 'If you can carry me to the water, I should have the strength to swim home. I know someone who makes potions.'

'I'll try.' But I wasn't convinced I could do it alone. I took Biscuit off his leash and told him to stay.

Close up, she smelled of sweat and brine; tiny crabs and shrimp moved in her matted hair like animated gifs. Her body was warm, her skin pink and blotchy. 'Sit up a bit?' I asked.

With my hands under her underarms, I tried to lift her, but she was even heavier than she looked. I could never do this by myself. My mind flew to Juliet. 'There's someone who might help. Is it okay to call her?'

'Sure. Get all your mates to gawp at me.'

'Not really a friend. She writes about mermaids.'

'Hmph.' She appeared unimpressed.

I phoned Juliet, who sounded surprised at my call. Without being specific, I got her to promise to be down on the beach ASAP. Then, while waiting, I took a bottle of water from my bag. 'Fancy a drink? There's a chocolate biscuit, too.'

'Yes, and yes. I'm starving.'

She gulped down the water, then ate the KitKat greedily. Her opened mouth revealed chocolatey teeth.

I spotted Juliet in the distance. She hurried over to us.

'Oh, it's you,' said the mermaid.

'Afraid so,' said Juliet.

'You two know each other?' I said, surprised.

'We do,' the mermaid said.

The tension was palpable, and I wondered what had happened there. 'She's responsible for the words in plastic on the beach,' I told Juliet.

'You are?' It was Juliet's turn to register surprise.

'Don't look so shocked,' said the mermaid. 'Not all of us make that stupid art.'

'Pre-Raphaelite art isn't stupid. It's wonderful,' said Juliet.

'Why do you want us *all* to be twee?'

I broke the silence that ensued with, 'She isn't well, Juliet. Help me get her back into the sea.'

'She's called Beatrice.' The mermaid pointed to herself. 'I'm Beatrice.'

'Beth,' I said.

'What's wrong, Beatrice?' asked Juliet.

'An infected cut. Now help me.'

Juliet and I bent down behind the mermaid's head, took one arm each, and heaved her a few metres before stopping for a breather. Excited at our shenanigans, Biscuit began barking. 'Shush,' I told him.

Juliet and I then dragged Beatrice another short distance.

'Careful,' she snapped. 'A pebble just dug into my back.'

Bit by bit, Juliet and I moved the mermaid closer to the sea, Biscuit following us and whimpering. By the time we got to the shore, a breeze was blowing, and the waves looked choppy.

'Get me right in,' ordered Beatrice.

I took off my shoes and socks; rolled up my trousers to my knees. Juliet did the same. In the water, cold sliced my feet. 'Brr.'

Still holding the mermaid's arms, Juliet and I waded in, until the sea was deep enough to bear her weight. By then, I was accustomed to the chill. As she lay on her back, able to float, the mermaid's face relaxed.

'Should be okay now,' she said.

'Do we get a thank you?' asked Juliet.

'Do something about all the plastic, for Christ sake.' Beatrice flipped onto her front and swam off, then dipped under the surface and reappeared a little further out. Looking back, she raised an arm out of the water. 'Thanks, Beth,' she called. 'And Juliet. You're still a jerk.' Then she dived under and vanished.

'Well, that told me,' Juliet said.

I wondered again what had happened between them. 'Think she'll be okay?'

'She's tough as old boots.'

We waded from the water, and I made a fuss of Biscuit. Then we picked up our shoes and socks and walked up the beach, both caught in our own thoughts. We sat down near the top, facing the sea.

'You knew her well?' I asked.

'Not really. When writing my book, I used to go up the coast in a small boat to photograph beach art, and I got friendly with a few mermaids. *She* wasn't the easiest.' Juliet's curt tone suggested a reluctance to say more. She brushed the sand off her feet and put on her socks and shoes. 'She's right about us doing more about the plastic.'

'Why not join in with the plastic picking?'

'That's like putting a Band-Aid over a bullet hole.' She thought for a minute. 'Do you have photos of *all* Beatrice's beach works?

I got out my phone and showed her.

'Great. Could you email these to me?'

'Sure. Why?'

'I'm thinking it's time to write an article for the papers about her art. Mermaids angry about plastic pollution is quite the story.'

'You didn't know about her kind of art?'

She avoided my eye. 'There have always been a few mermaids creating edgier work, but I never took it seriously. When I met Beatrice before, she was making these spindly sculptures out of fishbones and dead gull skulls. Creepy. I much prefer their traditional art.'

'Anything more I can do to help with the article?'

'No, but there is *something* you can do.'

'Yes?'

'A website for our local branch of the anti-plastic charity. The one you made for my books is brilliant.'

I hesitated—the last few hours of me-time a week would be gone. But an image flashed in my head of Beatrice's infected cut. If she'd risked her health protesting, couldn't I do more? Frannie calling me Mrs Ostrich flew to mind too; at least this would shut my daughter up. 'Go on, then. Why not.'

'We could call our branch the Friends of Mermaids.'

'Friends of Stroppy Mermaids.'

Juliet laughed. 'You've got her number.'

THE MUSHROOM LOVERS

After her bath, Bella notices a patch of grey-brown spots on her arm, the size of a 50p piece. The next morning, she wakes to find each spot has grown into the shape of a Chinese fan, 2cm wide. 'What on earth?' she gasps.

'Let's go to the doctor,' Button advises.

At the surgery later, Dr Khan stares. 'Never seen anything like it, but it's not a carcinoma. I'll refer you to a dermatologist.'

Despite it not being far, they opt for a taxi home. Button's arthritis is bothersome and Bella gets so tired since her double mastectomy last year. Raindrops speckle the taxi window, make the kerbs glint. Bella wonders, not for the first time, which one of them will die before the other. Her gaze drops to the growth on her arm and a shiver rises through her, making her heart speed up. Back at the flat, they sit together on their old green velvet sofa and drink a cup of hot chocolate while listening to Joni Mitchell's *Blue,* their favourite album.

The following day, more grey-brown fans poke from Bella's skin, each twice as wide as before and as thick as a knife handle. 'They're oyster mushrooms, aren't they,' she exclaims.

'Oh my goodness, yes,' he says.

They know this because they are keen amateur naturalists who used to run plant identification walks in the local parks. She uses a magnifying glass to examine the cream-coloured gills on the underside and then shakes her head in disbelief. 'How weird!'

'You know, oysters mainly grow on decomposing wood, Bella,' he says.

'Now isn't the time for your cheek, Button.'

He shrugs and grins in his playful manner.

They first coined their nicknames over sixty years ago, both chasing the last box of chestnut mushrooms on a market stall in London. 'Let me buy you a drink and it's all yours,' he'd said. They'd got drunk at The Duke of

Wellington pub and had given each other mushroom-themed names. He was Button because of his nose, and she was Portabella—later Bella—because she rented a bedsit on Portobello Road.

With worry prickling her, Bella carefully monitors how fast the thing on her arm is growing. A day later, the mushrooms extend past her elbow and almost halfway to her shoulder, and a spotty lump has appeared on her other arm.

'Me, too. Look!' He lifts his white *Peace and Guitars* t-shirt to reveal his flabby stomach. Near his belly button is a little patch akin to hers. He breaks off a mushroom and sniffs it. 'Should we cook them later?'

'Urgh, no. That's cannibalism, surely.'

'When life gives you oyster mushrooms, make stroganoff.' He chuckles.

She can't help but laugh, too. It's a relief to know his body is also sprouting fungi.

She makes them a mug of green tea each and puts honey in hers when she normally has none. He eats a flapjack, then another. 'I'm craving sugar,' he says.

'How odd. So am I.'

The living room is cluttered with keepsakes from their travels since retirement—engraved gourds from Bolivia, hand-painted ceramic mushrooms from Mexico. The walls hold photos of their life: at the Portobello flat, her in a minidress and beehive hairdo and him in a Beatles-style dress shirt; outside their first cottage in Maldon, with baby Chanterelle; arm-in-arm in Blakeney, where they took teenage Chanterelle to see the seals; Chanterelle with her husband in Costa Rica, where they work in conservation. Bella sips her tea, looking from photo to photo, reminding herself how blessed she has been.

In a matter of days, the mushrooms engulf her arms and upper torso. His swarm over his belly and down the side of both legs. She isn't unnerved anymore. Though she can't fathom why, she welcomes it.

'If I had a choice, I'd become a tree,' he says.

'And I'd become one right beside you.'

'Should we tell Chanterelle what's happening?'

'I've been wondering that, too, but let's leave it. We don't want to worry her when she's so far away.'

It isn't long before they no longer fit into clothes. She finds it hard to stand upright because of the fungi mass and waddles slowly. She is so tired that she forgets words. An earthy aroma follows her everywhere.

One night, Bella lifts her lids to see a phosphorescent, pale-lemon shimmer. It is as if they are both bathed in fireflies. She wakes him. 'Button. Look! We're glowing.'

He opens his eyes. 'Or perhaps we're radioactive,' he says and laughs.

They hold hands, marvelling at their luminosity. The bedroom is filled with earthly magic, enchanting the world.

In her dream, they're young again. She skips through a moonlit meadow with him.

When morning light spills into the room, the mushrooms have attached his left hand to her right. Conjoined, they get up and lumber to the kitchen. With her free left hand and his right, they make tea and then totter back to the bedroom with mugs and biscuits. She eases her stiff body down on top of the duvet and feels a twinge of dread.

'I'm actually scared,' says Bella.

'Don't be. We're in this together. Literally,' says Button.

Bella drifts in a honeyed state between sleep and wakefulness, too drowsy to lift her head for more than a few minutes. She dreamily registers the transition from afternoon to evening by the shift in light.

Amid the darkness, she opens her lids wearily, peering at her luminous Button through the mushroom pads on her cheeks. Or is that herself? Who knows where she ends and he begins?

Night dissolves, as does consciousness. Mycelium binds them into an organic obsolete oneness.

Ms Wiffle's Open Book

I never expected a book to spark fistfights in the village. It all started when an advert appeared on a postcard in the Co-op: *What's the most important thing YOU need to know? Consult Ms Wiffle's Open Book. Only £15. 22 Parkfield Road. 07700 900432*

As a retired chemistry teacher and a sceptic, I would normally have ignored this nonsense, but I lived at 27 Parkfield Road, so I was intrigued. I hadn't yet met the new tenant at 22. It was unclear what service was being offered, though fleecing the gullible with some kind of fortune-telling looked likely. At least it didn't cost a fortune. The name Ms Wiffle seemed more comic than clairvoyant.

A few days later, I bumped into a slim woman coming out of 22 Parkfield Road. She looked in her forties and wore a jogging kit and trainers. Her long copper hair was tied into a sleek ponytail, and her wide face featured big grey eyes. Not what I imagined a fortune teller to look like.

'Hello,' I said. 'Ms Wiffle?'

'Uh-huh.' Her gaze was direct.

'Allie Ceenick. I live over there with my cat Helium.' I pointed.

Her eyes smiled. 'Oh?'

'I saw your advert in the Co-op. What's this Open Book about?'

Maybe my tone revealed my scepticism because she said, 'Why not make an appointment and see,' with a hint of a grin. She sounded well-spoken. 'Bye,' she said and took off jogging.

Our quiet village by a river was of its time: one gastropub, one Co-op, one food bank, and four dog-walking services. Ms Wiffle quickly became known as someone polite who kept herself to herself. I Googled her out of curiosity and found she had no online presence. Rumours circulated that her mother had been wealthy, meaning she had an inheritance, and that she had spent years in spiritual development—some said in an ashram in Kerala, others said with shamans in Peru. When I bumped into Ms Wiffle, I inquired about her spiritual training.

'Spiritually evolved, me?' She coughed a laugh.

It was no surprise that Janey Foolscap, a woman up for anything, was the first of my friends to make an appointment. I assumed the Open Book would offer fortune-cookie-style advice. According to Janey, the guidance for her was oddly specific and uninspiring—no walking in Riverside Meadows for a week, without explanation. 'Fifteen quid down the drain,' said Janey. She ignored the advice, but four days later, I heard she'd been charged by a rogue cow in the meadows and had broken her leg.

More locals booked appointments. Elaine Mugwort received the message that her GP had made the wrong diagnosis. Her recent fatigue was due to post-covid problems and not her age. That also proved to be the case.

'Wasn't it merely an educated guess?' I asked when I ran into Elaine.

She leaned in close. 'No, Allie. The words actually appeared...' Then she clammed up, saying she'd promised Ms Wiffle to keep what happened in a session confidential.

Petra Redbull was warned to wear a bicycle helmet if she attended the *Just Stop Oil* march in London at the weekend. During the event, someone hurled a mug from a third-storey window at the protesters. It hit Petra's helmet, bruising her head; without the protective gear, it might have killed her. 'How the hell did the book predict that would happen?' said Petra later.

As Ms Wiffle's fame grew in the village, a divide opened between believers and non-believers. I fell into the latter camp and wasn't alone in wondering if she spent time sleuthing on social media, collecting information, or was a hacker. 'She must be a charlatan,' said Dr Parknose, the one who failed to identify Elaine's long covid. Others, especially those who'd become regular clients, defended Ms Wiffle to the hilt. Two elderly friends had a fierce row about her in the Co-op's fresh fruit aisle, and a dispute between pros and antis at the allotment almost ended in fisticuffs.

As division in the village grew, not everyone visiting Ms Wiffle did so with noble intentions. A clearer picture, therefore, emerged about what happened during a session. Ms Wiffle would seat the client at her kitchen table and fetch a red and gold embossed book the size of a dictionary. She then sat down herself and flicked through the hundreds of blank pages until a message—in comic sans font—appeared on one 'as if from nowhere'. She claimed she didn't know where the words came from and they materialised on a different page each time, vanishing as soon as the client left.

I assumed some trickery was involved, but what?

People from further afield came for consultations; the unknown cars regularly parked along our street irritated me. A journalist rang my doorbell one day, explaining that she was writing an article about Ms Wiffle; the psychic hadn't responded to nine left voicemails. I reluctantly agreed to answer a few questions, mostly saying, 'Sorry. I have no idea.' Afterwards, prompted by my guilt, I knocked on Ms Wiffle's door to warn her that the press was sniffing around.

She thanked me. 'God, they're so intrusive.'

After a well-known celebrity—whom I'd never heard of—came from London to consult Ms Wiffle, he praised her highly in *Hello* magazine. A few days on, two paparazzi with cameras parked on Ms Wiffle's doorstep. An hour later, my doorbell rang, and it was Ms Wiffle herself. She had pulled her hoodie hood up around her face. 'I've just got home from a walk. I don't think the press has clocked me yet. Can I please come in and hide here?'

I let her in and found out her first name was Willow.

'Willow Wiffle. Really?' I said.

'Yes.'

We both laughed.

We had a cup of tea, a slice of cake, and a chat. She came across as down-to-earth, the opposite of what I expected. 'Is the book from Tibet as I've been told?' I said.

'God, no. I bought it in a second-hand bookshop in Brighton and had no idea it'd have, well, unexpected powers. I only chose it as it looked good for doodling in.'

'Is that true?'

She shrugged. 'Sometimes I just feel like giving the thing away. It caused a massive hassle in the last place I lived, too. The truth stirs people up. I even had to change my name.'

'So you weren't Willow Wiffle originally?'

'Of course not.'

After a couple of hours and three cups of tea, she sighed and said she'd better go home, as it didn't look like the paparazzi were budging. I watched her stride past them to get to her door, ignoring their questions.

The paparazzi got bored and left by 6 pm, but at 9 pm music drifted up the street, and I looked out of the window to see John Fogglet outside her cottage, playing his guitar and crooning, 'I Will Always Love You'. When he'd finished, an upper window opened.

'Please go home,' called out Willow.

'But I love you.'

'I barely know you. Go away.' The window shut.

Later, after the pubs closed, a drunken argument erupted on the street outside, where half a dozen people were gathered.

'She's a charlatan,' cried a voice.

'Shut up. She's a miracle,' shouted another.

A fight broke out, and I called the police.

Two days later, Ms Wiffle's advert disappeared from the Co-op. I heard she was declining most requests for appointments, except for a few regulars. Some in the village moaned about this 'unfair favouritism', while others banged on her door, refusing to take no for an answer. On one occasion, I saw a limo pull up and the chauffeur got out. He shouted through Ms Wiffle's closed door that the popstar with him would pay a thousand pounds for a session, but she didn't respond.

The day that a removals van parked outside 22 Parkfield Road, I went into the street to investigate. The men told me Ms Wiffle had already left the village. They refused to say where they were taking her things.

Two weeks later, a hand-addressed, heavy parcel was delivered to my door with no return address. What was this? I opened it to find no card or note but something that felt like a hardback book, wrapped in gold and red paper. A shiver ran down my spine and I shoved it away in a bottom drawer, too uneasy to unwrap it.

BOOTLEG CHOCOLATE

I check the kitchen cupboard. *Shit!* Right out of dark chocolate. I need to get some more from the black market, but that can be dodgy, even dangerous, so first I'll psyche myself up with exercise.

My bike is propped against a wall in my large living room. I get on and start a circuit around a clutter-free track at the room's edge.

A stranger strides in from the garden, through the open French windows. Twenty-something and with long dark hair like mine, she asks what I'm doing. Odd people keep turning up and asking me stupid questions, but it doesn't faze me.

'I'm trying a bit of recycling.' I pedal past her, my heart pumping.

'It looks to me as if you're going round your room on a bike.'

'The council insists we recycle our waist. That's what I'm doing.'

She scoffs. 'Are you thick or do you tell crap jokes? And anyway, it's your W-A-S-T-E not W-A-I-S-T.'

Panting now, I halt the bike and frown. 'How come you know I said W-A-I-S-T?'

Her eyes narrow. 'Because your words are appearing on the air in front of your mouth, just for a moment. A bit like when you exhale in the freezing cold and can see your breath.'

'Shit. No way,' I say, and *Shit. No way,* materialises briefly near my lips. How long has this been going on and how come I never noticed it before? It's amazing how you can shimmy through life with obvious things eluding you.

'I get weird stuff in front of my mouth sometimes.' Her words crystallise into a tiny black cloud, from which letters rain one by one.

'What's that cloud of letters about?' I ask, deciding henceforth to ignore any words appearing in the air. Paying attention to them will drive me crazy.

'Perhaps because I'm always so sad.' She starts to cry.

'If you must blub, at least drip your tears on my cheese plant.' I gesture to the wilted thing in the corner. 'It hasn't been watered in ages. I get fined for doing that Something about water shortages due to global warning.'

'Global warming. It's M not N, idiot,' she says, and breaks down sobbing.

I say nothing but point at my cheese plant again. She moves across the room and positions her head to drop her tears on it, and relief flushes over me. I don't bother asking why she's so emotional. I'm not good with other people's problems. My ex would add, 'And that's an understatement'.

'I'm going,' wails the woman.

She strides into the hallway, and I hear the front door open and slam shut. She's probably annoyed I didn't ask what was wrong, but I can't deal with the psychological crap of random strangers. Life is too weird, anyway.

I prop the bike against the wall. I used to love riding round this city, but now gangs of marauding estate agents will drag you off the bike to steal it in broad daylight. Imagine! It's been like this ever since the petrol shortages, when cars were banned.

I'm still having serious pangs for chocolate. I put on my boots and denim jacket, open the hall cupboard, and take out eight arms of old mannequins, which I slip into a black holdall. When buying bootleg goods, you need to be well-armed. That sounds like a stupid joke, but it's true. The bootleg economy deals in arms—dolls' arms, mannequin arms, antique chair arms, sofa arms, monkey arms, even human arms. I'm aware of one bloke who gave his right arm for a dozen bars of organic Ecuadorian chocolate. Literally. Metaphors becoming concrete are part of life here.

After leaving the house, I hurry down Wire Street. The sun is putting in a half-arsed appearance, but it's not cold. I halt abruptly as a sheep falls out of the sky, lands— kerplunk!—on the pavement ten metres in front, then bounces back into the air. It's probably from the tall block of flats to the left, full of bored kids with nothing better to do than toss livestock. I walk on quickly. I don't want to be hit by a GM bouncing sheep today.

Towards the end of Wire Street, a slim woman with dark bobbed hair and a red coat approaches me. 'Hi,' she says, and stops. 'Do you fancy having a quick chat about Surrealism?'

'No.'

'Suit yourself,' she says calmly and strolls past me.

I turn onto Mile Road, which goes on for about a kilometre. At the end is a row of boarded up shops and a bank that is open. These businesses now deal in contraband goods: tea, coffee, chocolate, tampons, jelly beans, hoovers, bananas, hot water bottles, pet guinea pigs, rubber ducks. Money stopped being in wide circulation years ago, but the wheeler-dealer types who used to work in banks quickly found a new niche.

I should mention that most jobs here are paid in a mix of vegetable boxes, bags of flour, rent tokens and luxury bedclothes. So you often see graffiti around: LESS PYJAMAS MORE BANANAS or WE'RE EQUIPPED FOR BED BUT NOT FOR LIFE.

Anyway, I digress.

The bank is called ARE YOU SERIOUS? A guard is at the door. I know he's a guard because he's built like an ox. Plus, he's got the word GUARD tattooed on his forehead. I go up to him.

'Sorry, we're closed, miss,' he says.

'Why?'

'The place is under new management. It only opens on dates that are prime numbers.'

'Today's the eleventh. Eleven is a prime number.'

'The new management isn't good at maths, miss.'

I lean forward, saying in a quiet voice, 'Well, I need some dark chocolate.'

He folds his arms. 'No idea what you're talking about.'

Shit! I've stupidly contravened a basic rule of bootleg dealing. 'I mean, I want to take out a small loan for a bicycle,' I say, hurriedly backtracking. People *in the know* refer to chocolate using that phrase. I probably shouldn't be saying it in case any police read this, but then, I might be bullshitting, not giving away the *real* lingo for chocolate.

The guard opens the door and nods. 'Please go in.'

'But I thought you were closed.'

'We open on dates that are prime numbers. If I'm not mistaken, today's the eleventh.'

I stare at him, then shrug, and go inside.

At one desk, a young, slender woman with a blonde ponytail is typing on a keyboard. I clear my throat and she looks up.

'I'm looking to take out a small loan for a bicycle,' I say.

'Sorry, we don't arrange those anymore.'

'You're lying.'

'I am indeed lying.' She nods curtly. 'Come with me.'

She leads me down a staircase to the basement and then into a corridor lined with posters of luscious coffee beans and sensual chocolate bars. I stop and drool.

'Don't do that. Lechery disgusts me,' she says.

'Get over it.'

The narrow corridor, lit only by bare bulbs, goes on and on and on. We walk in single file, her before me. I'm surprised she keeps up the pace in those high heels; I'm grateful to be in trainers. It's cold here and I shiver. Smells a bit of mould, too. Glancing at my watch, I estimate we've been walking for ten minutes. 'How much longer?' I ask.

She turns her head back. 'Stop moaning.'

Twenty minutes later, with my feet starting to hurt, I say, 'How come it's so far? Last time, the small loans for bicycles were stashed in your secret attic.'

'Things change.'

Eventually—it takes fifty minutes—we go up some stone steps and come to a black door. It opens into a high-ceilinged room about thirty metres in length, with a black slate floor and narrow, floor-to-ceiling windows. The walls are all painted black and dotted with doors.

Dozens of black tables with goods on them are set up in rows. Men and women in dark clothes sit at the tables; some talk into black mobile phones, others deal with customers. Tiny black butterflies (probably genetic mutants caused by global warning) flit between ebony flowers growing from black pots.

'So this is the black market,' I say.

'How did you guess?' She leads me to a table. 'This is who we deal with. And it's where I leave you.'

'But how do I get home?'

'Not my problem.' She disappears into the crowd.

The black-suited, fat-jowled man behind the table nods. I tell him I want dark chocolate and open my holdall to show him the mannequin arms. He gives me a thumbs-up and takes two arms in exchange for eight bars of Ecuadorian 85% chocolate. I'm thrilled but keep a straight face—that's a cheap price, especially since this seems the black market of all black markets.

Wandering around at leisure, I buy two bags of ground coffee (for one mannequin arm), some sink unblocker, peaches, lemons, bin liners, and a packet of jelly beans. I slip them all in my holdall, grinning. I can't believe my luck—what a fantastic market! It's throbbing with more people than I've seen since the last Job Lottery.

I sit down at a table to play a quick game of Sugar Chess with an unshaven, curly-haired stranger. When you lose a piece, you eat it. It's not every day I get to watch some hot bloke scoff pawns, knights and bishops. He comments on all the sugar, though. 'Doesn't it make you sick?' he says.

'Stop moaning. Just play,' I say, and shove my queen in my mouth.

In reply, he checkmates me and smirks.

I stare at him and then eat my king, too.

I get up and stroll around the market, flicking a hand at the odd black butterfly bugging me. But suddenly there's wailing outside—a police siren. *Shit!* Heart racing, I glance about. Which way to go? The sellers and their bootleg goods vanish quickly through various black doorways, but I stand there frozen to the spot with my holdall.

The red-coated woman I met earlier appears, as if from nowhere, and beckons me with a long finger. 'Like to chat about experiments with fictional form?'

'Stop asking ridiculous questions, especially when I'm probably about to be arrested.'

She sighs and points to a door on the left. 'Try through there.'

I do—it leads down some stone steps and into a dimly lit, chilly corridor. I hurry along, wondering where the hell I'll come out, glancing behind occasionally to check no one has followed. Five minutes' brisk walk brings me to a crossroads in the corridor. I've no idea which way to go, so turn right. Twenty minutes later, I end up at a red door. Opening it, I ascend some steps into what seems to be a storeroom filled with tins, packets, recycled teddy bears, and plastic inflatable animals. Another door takes me into a shop—my local convenience store, in fact.

'Oi! What were you doing in my storeroom?' The owner holds up an inflatable swordfish as a weapon.

'Sorry, Mr Patel. My mistake.' I hurry out before he clobbers me. He's belligerent and armed with a fish.

Safely back home, I make some fresh coffee in a cafetière, leave it to brew, and then pour myself a large mug. It smells delicious. In the lounge, I sit on the sofa and take a sip of the beverage—it's good and strong.

I flick on the television. The live news is covering a police swoop on a black market. Hang on—it's the one I was just at. Christ, I still seem to be there. A close-up shot shows me holding some kind of furry arm and being arrested by a police officer.

It's not the first time I've somehow duplicated myself or been duplicated. I ran into a stroppy version of myself in the local hairdresser two months back and got into a terrible argument about hairstyles, but that's another story.

Watching my other self's arrest on television, I gulp down more coffee. Suddenly, I feel weird—my palms sweat, heart thuds, head goes faint. As if I'm falling, but there's nowhere to fall.

'Breathe deeply,' I say to myself in a stern voice. After a few lungfuls of air, I calm down. The odd experience was probably just a kick from all the caffeine, but I turn off the television just in case.

The brunette with the red coat steps into my living room through the French windows. 'Do you fancy talking about the death of realistic narrative?' she asks.

'No.'

She crosses her arms, raises her eyebrows.

'Sod off,' I add.

She shakes her head in disapproval and strides out into the hallway. When I hear the front door slam, I sigh with relief.

I eat a piece of the chocolate, letting it melt on my tongue. God, it's delicious—bitter with just a hint of fruit.

Then I try to work out how to end this story, but realise I have no clue. So from the side-table, I pick up a book on old album titles, shut my eyes, and open it at a random page. Raising my eyelids, I see that I've chosen:

Stop Making Sense.

Fox Freak

The first word Lis ever said was 'fox'. When she played on the lawn as a toddler, a family of foxes would sometimes gather by the apple tree at the end of the garden to watch. The biggest one—her mummy called him Reynard—would cock his head.

'Shoo,' her daddy would say, waving his arms. 'They're wild animals,' he told Lis. 'I want them nowhere near my little girl.'

'I don't get the sense they want to hurt our baby,' her mummy said.

Lis liked to stand at the French windows, gazing out at them. Sometimes, when her daddy wasn't there, Reynard crept up to the French windows to look in at her. 'Foxy fox. Foxy fox,' she'd say. After a time, he'd stroll away, and she'd stare at his big, beautiful tail.

She had a tail, too, no longer than a pencil, which matched her wavy auburn hair. She loved the *swish-swish* sound it made when she waggled it hard. Her parents called it her 'thing'. Mummy had sewn a pocket of material into the back of all her knickers for her to tuck it into, and she put her in loose dresses with wide skirts. 'You need to hide your thing because people can be mean, honey,' said her mummy.

Lis sometimes caught her parents talking about her, their voices drifting upstairs like ugly music when they thought she was asleep.

'Her damn thing,' her daddy would say. 'If only we could afford a private surgeon to remove it.'

'I'm gobsmacked you're even considering that. She's only a baby,' cried her mummy.

Up on the landing, Lis didn't really understand the words, only that she was the cause. She hurried back to bed and lay there, feeling the darkness falling on her.

***

Lis's parents didn't let her go to preschool: 'You're not ready to go anywhere without us.' They read stories to her, taught her nursery rhymes, and let her watch Dangermouse and Fraggle Rock on the television, but she spent a lot of time playing alone, too. She told herself tales about travelling to the moon, where little white swans gave her moon sherbet because they thought her tail was so lovely. She made picture after picture of stick-insect animals with four legs and bushy tails.

Close to Lis's fifth birthday, her mummy gave her a grey school skirt and a blue cardigan with the St Mary's primary school logo. 'Look what I got for you, honey.'

Lis's tummy fluttered with nerves, but she was also excited to start school and make some friends.

Her heart skipped when she saw the school playground with its climbing frames, wooden playhouse and hopscotch court. In the first week, when the children were doing leapfrog in P.E., Lis's tail slipped out of her knickers for all to see. Her face flushed hot as everyone stared, mouths agape. Later, like a pack of wolves, the other girls hunted her down in the playground; behind the playhouse, hands snatched at her, trying to lift her skirt to glimpse the tail.

'Don't,' Lis cried, muscles straining as she struggled to keep the skirt in place.

On Friday, when Lis was in the toilets, a gang of girls wrestled her to the floor. She fought back, pushing them off, but she was outnumbered. In no time, she found herself on her stomach on the hard floor, with a girl on each side pinning her arms. She squirmed as they tugged her knickers down and saw her tail. Emma, the ringleader, said, 'Urgh. You freak.'

Emma smirked at her friends, but Lis broke free of their grasp and made a perfect red score down Emma's face with her nails.

Emma howled as she ran from the toilets.

It was Lis who was told off. 'You cannot go around scratching your classmates,' the teacher said. 'Do you understand?'

Lis tried to explain, but the unfairness of having to defend herself caught in her throat, silencing her.

Throughout that term and the one after, the bullying continued. 'Fox freak, fox freak,' Emma and her gang jeered. Sometimes Lis blanked out their words by imagining herself in a wood; she conjured in her mind the trees around her, the easy greens and browns, the earthy smell. At other times, something snapped in her, and she hissed and scratched at the bullies. Her parents talked to her teacher on several occasions and told Lis they'd written to the school board, too. The headteacher ticked Emma and her gang off, but also called Lis alone into her office and stared down at her. 'You must learn to control your wild temper, Lis. And make more effort to fit in.'

Back at home, worries stuck to Lis' thoughts like torn-up crepe paper to glue. She drew big circles on paper and coloured them in with thick black crayons, and in the centre of the dark pools, she drew tiny orange foxes.

Eventually, her parents found her a place at a village primary school. There, the other kids never asked Lis to join in with their games of tag or Simon Says, but neither did they bully her. She liked to stand at the edge of the school playground, staring through the wire fence, over the grassy field, and towards the woods in the distance. The wildness called to her.

***

On the first day of secondary school, Lis sat hunched at the back of the classroom of thirty unknown faces. At break time, a girl approached her and said, 'I've got Jamaican jerk chicken in my lunch box. Want to sit and eat with me?'

Lis's heart lifted. 'Love to.'

Jamila was a skinny, big-hearted girl who enjoyed playing the flute and doing sports. The two friends discovered they both loved making up stories and play-acting roles—Ogg and Nogg, two stone-age girls who hunted bison; Zizz and Vizz, two alien explorers from the planet Moonbeam.

The bullying reared its head again because rumours about the tail spread quickly. Beaker Johnson and his mates from Year 9 took a particular interest in Lis and Jamila. When the girls passed them in a corridor, the boys made barking noises and asked, 'Did your mum shag a fox?'

Beaker saved his meanest antics for when Lis was alone, though, because Jamila's reputation as a fast runner gave her some kudos. Once, when Lis headed down the locker-lined corridor towards the school exit, some Year 9 boys burst out laughing. She had no idea why until she found a long piece of orange fake fur stuck to the back of her duffle coat. She ripped it off, her cheeks burning with humiliation.

At home, she cried, 'I want my tail cut off.'

'That's not possible,' said Mummy. 'We looked into surgery when you were about seven, but it can't be done on the NHS. Private cosmetic surgery costs thousands.'

'But I hate it.'

'I'm sorry, honey. We can't afford it.' Her mummy came close. 'Let me give you a hug.'

Lis pulled away. 'No! I just want the thing gone.'

After two reprimands by the headteacher and a suspension from school, Beaker stopped his bullying. Lis was left with fearful barbs around her heart, which hindered her attempts to befriend other kids. Kind, sensible Jamila made more friends, but Lis was like a lone fox skulking along a road in the dark.

One evening, during a sleepover at Jamila's house, Lis summoned the courage to show her tail. It was thickly furred, fox red, and the length of a ruler now; she had no idea how long it would eventually grow. Jamila had caught glimpses of it, never the entire thing. 'Swear not to tell anyone,' said Lis.

'I swear.' Jamila's eyes widened. 'It's so cool, like a small fox tail. Can I touch it?'

'Yes.'

'Oo. It's soft.'
'Watch this.' Lis wagged it.
'Wow.'

Showing her tail made Lis feel light and airy, but with a prickle of guilt, too.

Lis struggled at schoolwork while Jamila did exceptionally well. Lis was only good at art and music, but she worked hard at those subjects. The art teacher, who admired her paintings of half-human critters in spooky woodlands, encouraged her to enter competitions. Lis took up the alto saxophone after being transfixed by a Courtney Pine song, 'Children of the Ghetto', on the radio. She practised daily and got into the school orchestra; Jamila played near her on the flute. Lis's hearing was pitch-perfect. She became so accomplished that the teacher gave her solos, and Lis cherished how music lifted her spirits. With the saxophone mouthpiece between her lips, life pulsed through her.

When not playing it or doing her art, though, Lis felt adrift. A thorn of jealousy pricked her when she saw how Jamila fitted in and came top of the class. It didn't matter how well Lis did because all the other kids talked about was her tail. *I'm a freak,* she told herself.

***

After their GCSEs, Lis and Jamila moved together to the sixth-form college. Jamila took sciences while Lis studied arts subjects. A schism formed between them when Jamila began dating Freddie Chan, a cheerful lad who played piano in the college jazz band and waved his hands about as if conducting the conversation. Lis grew resentful that Jamila was spending so much time with Freddie.

Lis picked petty fights with her best friend. When Jamila played her latest CD, Lis said, 'Blur are rubbish.'

'I thought you liked them.'

'They are so last year.'

'Why are you so grumpy lately?'

Lis knew she was causing the tensions but couldn't stop herself. The friends spent less time together.

Lis began dressing in baggy black sweatshirts and hand warmers; flared purple skirts over ripped tights; dark lipstick and ebony nail polish. Her clothing hid both her shape and her tail. She disliked her lack of hips and non-existent bust. Her nose and chin were too long and pointed for her to be pretty. Frowning at herself in the bedroom mirror, she practised covering her mouth with a hand. Those vulpine eye-teeth peeking out over her lips—Lis couldn't afford to smile.

Lis had crushes on two boys at the sixth-form college, and Jamila suggested she ask them out. 'What have you got to lose?'

Plenty, actually. One boy blushed and said, 'Sorry, I'm busy.' The other looked at Lis as if she was a leech crawling up his leg. 'I'm not dating a freak.'

Lis's unhappiness erupted into quarrels with her parents. When her dad forbade Lis to have her nose pierced, she threw a hissy fit.

'I mean it. No nose piercings,' Dad said.

'Why can't *I* choose what I look like?'

'You don't get a say while you're still at school.'

'You're a control freak.'

'Go to your room.'

Lis shut herself in her bedroom, banging the door closed. She tossed the framed photo of her as a smiling toddler with her parents into the bin.

On weekends, Lis would tell her mum she was going to Jamila's. Instead of turning right into Jamila's street, Lis would ride her bike up the left-hand path to a wood on the outskirts of town. It was a small expanse of oak trees next to agricultural land, at its heart a circular clearing with one gigantic oak. Magic seemed to pulse here, and sunlight filtered through the leafy canopy, painting piebald patches of light and dark on the ground. She sat with her back to the oak and played tunes on the saxophone, then smoked roll-ups. Foxes would appear from the shadows to listen to her music. Sometimes having them as an audience sent heat radiating through her chest; at other times, she'd dump the instrument down and shout, 'Piss off.'

One summer evening, Lis was the lead saxophonist at a college jazz concert. Afterwards, Tom Hapless swaggered up to her. 'You were great, Lis,' he said.

She stared, surprised that he even knew her name. They'd never exchanged a word before. The broad-shouldered hunk had a long dark fringe; his emerald eyes, framed by thick lashes, gleamed with sensual promise. He had a reputation for breaking hearts.

'I wondered if you'd like to go out sometime?' he said.

'You mean... on a date?'

His grin seemed genuine. 'Would that be so terrible?'

Her heart caught in her throat. 'No. I mean, yes, yes, I'd like to.'

On the date, Tom was friendlier than she'd imagined, asking her about her love of music and complimenting her on her outfit. They took a stroll and sat on a bench, finding a shared taste in bands and singers.

'Do you know Bjork?' Tom asked. 'She's cool.'

'Yes, she's daring. Do you like Hyperballad?'

He nodded and grinned.

'The music on that track sounds like an ocean crashing on the rocks,' she said. 'It kinda echoes the lyrics.'

'You say cool things.'

That he didn't kiss Lis made her chew at her lip, but he invited her on a second date. He took her to the ghost house this time, an abandoned building on the outskirts of town where older teenagers sometimes hung out. It was Lis's first time there. The scuffed floor was littered with stained mattresses, empty bottles, and a tatty sofa; one mattress had a used condom on it, and the place reeked of mould. Why had he brought her here?

'Not the most hygienic place,' he said, 'but I like it because you can be alone. I can't escape enough from my family.'

'Me neither.'

Tom sat on a sofa, got out cans of beer from his

rucksack, and handed her one. He took out a little camera, too.

'Why have you brought that?'

His gaze darted to the wall. 'I like to take snapshots of this place. It looks like the hangover of a wild party.'

'Or a pit stop on the way to the apocalypse.'

He laughed.

She retrieved her tobacco pouch. 'Fancy a cigarette?'

'Why not?'

She rolled both of them one. They complained about their families as they swigged beer and smoked. She liked how he closed his eyes for a moment after inhaling, as if savouring the tobacco. She imagined how his lips felt to the touch.

He confessed to his hatred of his father, a bully.

'I hate bullies, too,' Lis said.

He fiddled with the leather bracelet on his wrist.

When they were tipsy, he said, 'You're so interesting. How come you don't have a boyfriend?'

She blushed. No one had ever said such a thing to her. He extended his hand to touch her face with a finger before leaning towards her mouth.

Her first ever kiss. Just their lips touched. Was she doing it right? It was over in a flash.

'Sorry. Shouldn't have.' Tom smiled. 'Couldn't help myself.'

'Let's do it again.'

The second kiss was longer. Afterwards, her lips tingled with pleasure.

'That was nice.' He slid his arm around her shoulders. 'There's something I'd like to ask.'

'What?'

He glanced down. 'I probably shouldn't.'

'Go on. I'm intrigued.'

'I'd, well—I'd like to see your tail.'

She tensed in fear.

'The idea of it is a complete turn-on.'

She tried to read his face, to figure if he was being genuine.

'Please, Lis?'

She shook her head. 'Not today.'

'Sorry for asking. I hope I haven't blown things, and you'd want to come back here with me again.'

'I'd like that.'

They arranged another date for the following Tuesday. Over the weekend, she fantasised about him constantly, and her heart thrummed. At school on Monday, however, Freddie and Jamila took her aside and told her they'd heard Tom had made a bet with his friends that he could photograph Lis's tail. He intended to share the photo with his mates.

Lis was unsure whether to believe them.

'I promise I'm not lying,' said Jamila, as if reading her mind.

'I don't understand. He seemed so nice.'

'Did he ask to see your tail?' said Freddie.

Lis's chest went cold as she nodded.

'Some boys will say anything to get what they want,' said Freddie.

Lis's mood swung like a pendulum from anger to shame and back. On Tuesday, she summoned the courage to confront Tom and she first told him she wasn't keen to go back to the ghost house.

'Why not? It was fun last time, wasn't it?' he said.

She didn't reply.

'Is anything wrong?'

'I... I'm told you have a bet on.'

His eyes dropped to the pavement. 'I don't know what you're talking about.'

'They said you want to photograph a part of me.'

His cheeks flushed puce. 'Who said that?'

'Is it true?'

'I can't believe you're accusing me—'

'So it's not true?'

He spun around and strode away.

'The pig,' she muttered.

She hurried home, tears streaming down her face. Lis prayed he might phone her to say she was mistaken, but no call came. That night, hot with humiliation, she shaved all the hair off her tail. Without its fur, it was like a pathetically thin, boney rope.

Lis spent more time in the clearing in the woods. Loneliness swallowed her up, and the days limped past in a listless blur. Life seemed to have folded in on itself. The only thing that gave her pleasure was reading prospectuses from art colleges. The local Institute had a good reputation, but wouldn't it be better to apply to Falmouth or Goldsmiths?

One day in the clearing, she was midway through playing 'Smells like Teen Spirit' on the sax when she sensed someone approaching. She stopped. A solid black camera with a long lens pointed at her. Behind it was a thin, pale girl with long blue hair, DM boots, and dark leggings. The girl lowered the camera and came forward 'I was enjoying that.'

'Why were you taking my photo?' Lis snapped.

'Your face was kinda painted in this flickering light and shadow from the tree above. You looked romantic.'

Lis appreciated the girl's words, but were they sincere?

'You deserve a better audience than a few crows.'

'The foxes listen sometimes.'

The girl cackled, thinking it was a joke.

Lis enjoyed the unfettered sound of the laughter. 'The oaks are partial to a bit of sax, too.'

'Surely oaks would be more into Mozart or something.'

It was Lis's time to laugh. She then retrieved her cigarette papers. 'Fancy a roll-up?'

The girl shook her head. 'I'd rather you play that Nirvana song again.'

'You like Nirvana?'

'I'm called Frances, the same as Kurt Cobain's daughter.' The girl sat down. Her skin was pale, almost white.

As Lis played, the girl listened, closing her lids as if concentrating on an inner landscape the music conjured. Frances had a long, slender neck and dark eyes.

'That was so cool. Do you play in a band?'

'A jazz band. Do you often go out photographing alone?'

'I'm doing photography as part of my art foundation course at the Institute.'

'Really? I'm thinking of applying there next year.'

'I love the course.'

The two girls started hanging out. They enjoyed long walks, photographing lichen on gravestones and peeling paint on old doors. They saw the bands Urban Species and Morcheeba at the Arts Centre. Lis found it hard to trust the happiness infecting her. She daydreamed about Frances's elegant neck and the swan tattoo on her slender wrist.

One summer evening, Lis confessed to Frances about her dating disaster with Tom. 'Have you had many boyfriends?'

'I'm, er, into girls, actually.'

Delight filled Lis's lungs so quickly she could hardly breathe.

Frances picked at a fingernail. 'There's something I kinda need to say, Lis. I hope it doesn't mess up our friendship.'

'What?'

'I like *you* a lot.'

'Oh, my god. I like you too,' gushed Lis. Then came a jolt of fear. 'But... there's something I should tell you.'

'What?'

Say it, she told herself. 'I have a tail. A fox's tail.' Lis watched Frances's face carefully for a response.

Frances said nothing. Instead, she slipped her boots off and peeled her socks off, too.

Lis's shoulders tensed. What was Frances up to?

'Wanna know my secret?' Two bare feet were stuck out, and the toes wiggled. Frances had pale pink webbing toe-to-toe. 'See? I have a swan's feet.' She beckoned with a finger, murmuring, 'Come here, foxy fox.'

And Lis's heart hummed.

The Blind Ark

Out there were the shipping lanes, where tankers shuttled goods across the sea. Barry Blind approved of globalised trade—Kiwi fruit, iPads, BMWs, moccasin slippers, all transported efficiently, continent to continent. He breathed in, sniffing the air. It smelled faintly of seaweed and—what?—something he couldn't put his finger on, something disconcerting. The clusters of grey clouds gathering on the horizon unsettled him, too. *Should we have sold the house in Haslemere? Was buying The Blind Ark rash?*

Those questions again.

He picked up a black pebble shaped like a crescent moon and turned it over in his long, thin fingers before slipping it into his pocket. He checked his watch—he'd been walking for well over an hour—and headed back with a sigh.

At the Capescape Marina fence, a tall, steel structure topped by barbed wire, he greeted the stocky security guard.

Joe Patten unbolted the gate. 'Pleasant walk, Mr Blind?'

'Yes, thanks. Almost got to the end of the beach.'

'Be careful. Some GaiaNow! yobs were spotted right down there yesterday.'

'Don't worry. I'll be fine.' Barry continued into Capescape Marina. He'd always held a zero-tolerance policy towards risk in life. A stroll all the way along his local beach, together with living on *The Blind Ark*, were his two minor concessions to danger.

As he approached the wide concrete jetty where *The Blind Ark* was moored, his chin dipped. He'd hoped the twenty-five-metre luxury yacht would be a comfortably adventurous manner to spend his early retirement years, but six weeks in, it fitted him like a pair of expensive leather shoes that looked impressive but pinched painfully.

He glanced up. Ahead was Barbs in that chiffon

turquoise summer dress she'd bought yesterday. Even after decades of marriage, the sight of her could still set his heart racing sometimes. 'Hey, you,' he said. 'That outfit looks great.'

'Nice, isn't it?' Beneath a straw sun hat, her grey-blue eyes glimmered.

'Where are you off to?'

'A quick frappuccino.'

'Isn't "frappuccino" the Italian word for "overpriced drink"?'

'Isn't your middle name "Penny-Pincher" not Peter?' She winked.

Barry grinned—he appreciated her teasing him—and headed onto the yacht.

On deck, Barry stared out to sea, a slight wind prickling his face. The vastness of the ocean perturbed him, but touched something within him, too. The dark-grey waves were insistent, rhythmic. *Is the sea drumming out some warning through its waters?* A shiver slid down his neck. *What an odd thought.*

At his mahogany desk in the study, he settled to read *The Telegraph*, including a long article about the flaws of climate change science. He thought about Anna, who scoffed at his choice of paper, insisting that the climate crisis wasn't doom-mongering. This was one of their rituals: he'd furrow his brow, run his finger and thumb down his jaw, and she'd ask: 'Why do you buy that crap, Dad? You're not stupid. Can't you see fossil fuels are destroying the planet?' Words that came back to him when he saw grim television scenes of the latest floods in Somerset or Norfolk.

Barry blocked out Anna's voice, put down the newspaper, and gazed out of the window.

'Hey B.'

He twisted his head abruptly. 'Back already, Barbs? You almost made me jump.'

'It's only me.' Barbs strolled over to a shelf and screwed her nose up at the line of pebbles and shells on it. 'Bit grubby this lot. Not like you.'

'They make me feel close to the sea.'

Her laughter was sparkly. 'We're on a yacht. How much nearer do you want?'

'I was thinking. Why don't we take *The Blind Ark* out for a couple of days? Hire a few men to crew?'

'Absolutely not,' she said. 'I thought we'd agreed. Yachts are perfect to live on, but no sailing anywhere.'

'But I've been wondering—'

'No buts.' She approached him, reaching to take his hand. She stroked the side of it gently with her thumb, something she did when affectionate. 'Let's have lunch. I bought prosciutto Toscano. I'll whip up a minted melon salad to go with it.'

The prosciutto was his favourite. 'Sounds good.' He followed her to the kitchen, still frustrated by her attitude to sailing.

Shouts in the distance interrupted lunch in *The Blind Ark*'s sky lounge. Two dinghies were nearing the marina entrance. Barry grabbed the binoculars. A dozen people were on board each; some had dreadlocks and colourful tee shirts—purple, azure blue, and moss green. A bare-chested, tanned man stood with his hand in the air. Barry's shoulders tensed.

'Not refugees, is it? Not here,' said Barbs.

'Look more like GaiaNow!'

'Bloody hippies.' She picked up the binoculars and looked. Her brow furrowed. 'Right. I'm calling Security.' She put down the binoculars and dialed on her mobile. 'Mr Patten? Mrs Blind here. I need to report... Oh, you know?...' She nodded several times. 'Why not the police?... Oh... Now? Okay, then.'

She hung up and told Barry that they had to go to the quayside if they wanted to be kept updated.

On the quayside, Joe Patten stood at the edge of a group of residents, talking on his phone. Beads of sweat popped from Barry's brow, the hot sun glittered on the sea.

'Listen up,' called Joe, coming off his mobile. 'The coastguard will be here soon.'

'You think they're dangerous?' Barbs pointed towards the dinghies.

'They're just yobs, Mrs Blind,' said Joe. 'Don't you worry.'

The two boats were now within the marina. Large banners were unfurled and held up between them: *The Have-Yachts and Have Nots* and *How the Other Half Dies: Poverty Kills*.

'Oh, for God's sake. If they don't want to be poor, they should damn well get a job,' said Barbs. 'I will not feel guilty about having a yacht. I will not. Barry and I worked hard all our lives.'

'That first banner's got a decent pun,' said Barry.

'Barry!' She glared.

What did these people want? Barry's attention was drawn to how vast the sea was behind the dinghies. Glints of sunlight on the water reminded him of knives.

The coastguard arrived. As the vessels were guided away, shouting—and laughter—floated from on board.

***

As summer spun into autumn and the nights grew darker, Barry experienced an unease that crept upon him like mist from the sea. He ventured further off during the day, to the cliff tops beyond the beach. He picked up lost or discarded things and carried them back to his office. One day, he came across a pearly pink plastic octopus two inches long and a silver, turquoise earring. At home, he cleaned them up and placed both on a shelf.

Barbs spent more time at the Capescape beauty salon, gym, and mall, often returning with shopping bags. She shopped for clothes and jewellery online, too. When yet another delivery arrived, Barry asked what she'd bought.

'Hmm.' She examined the package. 'From Boden. I think these are pinafores I ordered for the girls.'

Surely Anna, their mum, wouldn't be keen on more clothes. 'Ensure you keep the receipts.'

'What's the point of having money if we can't spoil our grandkids?'

He was uncertain where she stored all the stuff she bought, but he sometimes heard her brisk footsteps go down to the lower deck at night.

Barry missed the discipline and preoccupation of work. His skills had been in capital budgeting and cost analysis. A first-rate bean counter. What was he now? A has-been bean counter—a second-rate pun?

And Barbs? She'd sold her successful, high-end catering business and toasted to 'a new life', but he'd find her in the sky lounge at 5 pm, clutching a cocktail, staring at Facebook.

'Are you okay, Barbs?' he asked.

'Fine,' she said and knocked back the last of her drink. 'Fancy a tipple? I'm going to treat myself to another.'

'Bit early, isn't it?'

'We're retired. We can drink when we like.'

She then took to sleeping in a separate cabin, and he missed going to bed with her. 'Does my snoring keep you awake?' he asked.

Her eyes looked bloodshot. 'I'm just finding it hard to sleep.'

'Try the blog Anna emailed me about ocean acidification. That will knock you out.' He grinned, expecting an amusing retort, but she turned away, her mouth scrunched down at the corners.

They used to enjoy dinners full of chat and good humour. Now Barbs picked at her food and fiddled absent-mindedly with the pearls on her necklace as if turning over unanswerable questions.

'This is delicious,' he said one evening, trying to make conversation. 'What's in it again?'

She prodded it with a fork. 'It's a confit of salmon with crab crush & dill drizzle.'

'Thought you liked this dish?'

She put her cutlery down. 'To be honest, I'm a bit fed up with salmon.'

'Is everything okay, Barbs?'

'Still not sleeping well, but it'll pass.'

'Why not see the GP? She might prescribe you something to help you get off.'

'I'll give it a week.'

After the meal, he retreated to his study to listen to Classic FM. His foot tapped, not to the music but from unfamiliar nerves. Their marriage had been through rough patches, particularly when Anna was a teenager, but he'd largely considered it a good one. He admired her strong-mindedness and snappy comebacks and the exquisite care she put into food and their home. They'd both been so busy with work for the previous two decades, though, that they'd not spent that much time alone together. Was being on a yacht healthy for them?

As bleak November began and the couple became more confined to the yacht, his collecting assumed a manic hue. He picked up more things from the clifftops, ignoring the inner voice that asked, *What are you doing?* When the days were too cold to walk far, he searched for antique bargains on eBay or toured the junk and antique shops in nearby towns.

During an aimless stroll on the lower deck, he discovered the cabin they used for storage was brimming with cardboard boxes. In one, he found piles of silk scarves and hand-blown glass ornaments; in another was a stack of child-sized fleece onesies. He trotted up to the main deck. 'There's no room left in the storage cabin, Barbs.'

'Really?' Her face reddened, and she folded her arms. 'Why don't we get rid of the beds in the second guest cabin? Fill it with cupboards and trunks.'

'But the grandkids sleep there.'

'They can use camping mattresses in the saloon or sky lounge. Much more fun.'

'Just looked in some of your boxes. What's with the fleece onesie fetish?'

She fidgeted with her wedding ring. 'Don't be silly. Just presents for the girls.'

Mail-order cupboards and trunks arrived. Whenever

Barry, coming home with a modest antique purchase, met Barbs, he'd blush and hurry to his study. He'd sit there, heart thrumming, wondering why he felt ashamed. *Collecting things isn't a crime.*

They bumped into Joe on the quay, his hands fisted on his hips, his brow wrinkled. 'You know, *The Blind Ark*'s a couple of feet lower in the water than *Victoria's Wave.* What've you got on it, Mr and Mrs Blind, a pair of hippos?' he said.

Barbs barked a nervous laugh. 'Don't be daft.'

The Blinds curbed their buying habits for a few weeks. Then violent storms struck southern England. The rain teemed down for four days; splits of lightning arced across the sky at night. While the Capescape yachts escaped damage, the scenic villages just inland were left calf-deep in water. When they'd moved to the boat, they also bought a rental cottage as an investment. They visited to survey the destruction. 'How awful,' said Barbs, her face ashen. 'Let's prepare ourselves thoroughly.'

'Yes.' Barry put an arm around her, uncertain of what she meant. Seeing the silt-sodden mess made a crack open up between the world he knew and a more brutal, uncompromising one he barely knew existed.

The following day, she came home with a camping stove, forty tins of soup, a 5 kg bag of rice, and swimming floats. 'For the cottage or yacht?' he asked.

'The yacht.'

Barry soon added to the items with a machine for purifying seawater, which he purchased online, and books from the local bookstore. He normally read crime capers but found himself hoarding dystopian novels. In his study, he whispered the titles as if they were mantras—'*Cloud Atlas...Riddley Walker...Oryx and Crake*'—and stared at his reflection in the mirror. *Who do these bleak books make me?* Someone else was looking out of his eyes, he realised, someone less essential, more apprehensive than him. A shiver slid down his back.

One Tuesday, near the marina, he spotted a couple on a

beach. The woman had dyed blue hair, the man dreadlocks, and tattoos covered the man's arms. Probably GaiaNow! Barry pulled out his mobile as a precaution.

The woman fell. Had she tripped? The man lurched forward, catching her, and laid her down gently. Barry hurried over. 'Is she alright?'

'She fainted. Does it often.'

Barry hesitated, then knelt beside her. *She's so thin.* Her young, wind-burnt face had chiselled cheekbones like Anna's. Her purple sweat top was flecked with dirt, and she smelled of something musty, maybe incense. 'Is she ill?'

'Just hungry.'

'Not had breakfast?'

'No. Money's tight.'

'Really?'

The man shot Barry a sharp look and then stroked the woman's cheek. 'Skye,' he said. 'Skye, honey.'

She sat up slowly. Her eyes were like penny-shaped pieces cut from the sky.

Barry got out a cereal bar from his rucksack. 'Why not eat something?'

'Thank you.' She tucked in voraciously. The man stared at the food, so Barry handed him an apple, which he wolfed down. They seemed starving.

The woman stood up. She shook his hand and her wide smile revealed wonky front teeth. 'I'm Skye.'

'Barry.' On impulse, he retrieved the thirty pounds from the wallet he carried with him on walks; there was never a lot of cash in it. 'Please treat yourselves to lunch '

'That's kind, but we can't accept it,' she said.

'I have more than enough money.'

The man accepted it. 'Thanks, mate. We'll do a shop at Lidl.'

As the couple set off along the beach, Barry stared after them. Could he have helped more?

He vowed to stop buying so much. As he tucked down to sleep that night, the image of Skye's thin face came to him and then morphed into Anna's.

One day, he found an article online about The Great Pacific Garbage Patch, a floating island of plastic refuse twice the size of Texas. *How haven't I heard about this before?* The article said there were four other huge garbage patches in various oceans. His foot tapped nervously.

His resolve not to buy lasted a fortnight. As the days got shorter and darker—and after winning a Regency teapot on eBay for a bargain—he began to shop again. In lucid moments, he'd wonder if this was a compulsion, an addiction, feeding a deep, unhealthy need. Then he'd spot a charming Victorian toy—a tin boy who climbed up and down a ladder—and think what harm was there in having it?

For Christmas, Barbs and Barry stayed with Anna in her cottage in Wivenhoe. It was a moderately uneventful festive period in Barry's reckoning; Barbs only argued twice with her daughter.

'You buy Rose and Ellie way too much, Mum,' said Anna on Boxing Day.

'You were always an ungrateful child.'

'I'm neither a child nor ungrateful.' Anna's brow creased. 'Why the need anyway?'

Barbs fiddled with her bracelet. 'What?'

'To spend money all the time.' Anna spread out her arms.

'What are you talking about?'

'That boat's brimming with stuff. I found roomfuls last time I was there.'

'When do you even visit us?'

'Mum! We came at half term.' Anna stared. 'Do you think you shop to avoid facing things?'

'Stop being ridiculous.' Barbs' mouth tightened into a hard line.

'And what about the carbon footprint of it all?'

'Not this again.'

'Don't look at me like that. It's not your future that's being destroyed—it's Rose's and Ellie's.' Anna's voice rose in pitch.

'I can't deal with this at Christmas.' Barbs strode from the room, and Barry went after her.

In the small children's playroom that doubled as a guest room, Barbs was red-faced. 'Anna's impossible.'

'She's strong-minded, just like her mother,' he said.

Tears welled in Barbs' eyes. 'Oh, B. It hasn't been a good Christmas, has it?'

It was the first time she'd called him B for ages. 'It's okay, Barbs. Come here.' He put his arm around her and drew her into a hug. As they stood embracing, he stared out of the window at the lime tree, stark against the low winter light.

'I'm sorry I'm so strong-minded sometimes,' she said.

'It's simply who you are, Barbs. I... I think Anna might be right about us buying too much, though.'

'Don't you start, too, B. It's nothing—just something I enjoy.'

The following morning, Anna sought out her father. 'I'm worried about you and Mum.'

'No need.'

'All that stuff on the yacht. You've hardly any room to breathe.'

'It's not that bad.'

'It is. Stop her shopping. It's like an addiction. Give things away. Learn to sail or scuba-dive instead.'

'I doubt your Mum will agree.'

'Talk to her.'

'She doesn't listen, Anna. You know that better than anyone.'

'Please try talking to her. Please.' She hugged him tightly, as if he were her child.

A phrase of hers looped through his head, one with a hint of poison in it: *it's like an addiction.*

***

Throughout a freezing January, the online sales offered Barbs sanctuary. 'I can never resist a bargain,' she said, as she directed two delivery men to place a large fridge in a corner of *The Blind Ark*'s sky lounge.

'Do we *really* need this?' asked Barry.

She scowled. 'It's for the drinks.'

Barry clenched his teeth. Barbs had always liked being in control, but previously her no-nonsense sharpness and humour meant he enjoyed surrendering. Now she was merely brittle and remote. *What's happening? Can I stop it?* These thoughts stalked him into the night.

Barry woke up at 2 am. What had disturbed him? Noise outside? Music? He slipped on boots and a fleece and trotted up to the deck. In the distance drum beats and a throbbing bass line echoed. *Who's there?* The music reverberated through the air, reminiscent of a primitive warning. A crescent moon threatened like a scythe in the dark. The vault of the night sky suddenly made him shiver. It was vast while he seemed tiny and of little consequence in comparison. Before, he'd always considered himself of moderate significance. But was he? He returned to bed, tossing before he got to sleep.

The next morning, Joe Patten refused to open the gate. 'The police want you all to avoid the beach for now. Those GaiaNow! hooligans held a party there last night. The police broke it up. Lots of arrests.'

Barry wondered if Skye and her boyfriend were there and if they were still malnourished.

Online, he found an article about GaiaNow! in *The Guardian*. It said they weren't an organised anarchist group, as was sometimes stated, but a loose association of people who campaigned against poverty, inequality, the shortage of affordable housing, environmental pollution, and climate change. Many, it continued, lived in caravans or even cars and struggled to make ends meet in recession-hit England; some wore dreadlocks and bright clothes as a nod to 1990s rave culture—these people, too, liked to party outside. *The Telegraph,* however, insisted that GaiaNow! were work-shy anarchists who claimed benefits while working casually.

Feeling a headache coming on, Barry massaged his eyebrows with his thumbs. It wasn't just that he was tempted to believe *The Guardian*. It was that everything felt uncertain and unmoored. He'd once been so clear about who he was and what he thought. Had he been deluding himself? Now his self seemed riddled with gaps, adrift without a compass. A hot tear pricked the corner of his eye. He squeezed his eyes shut. What should he do?

Firstly, get away from the yacht.

At supper, Barry suggested they take a trip to Bruges.

'Good idea, but I need new outfits first,' said Barbs.

'You've got more clothes than anyone could want.'

'But pastels are in, my dresses are too bright.'

'Well, buy something and I'll book the tickets.'

She stroked the side of his hand, which she hadn't done in months. 'Bruges will be lovely. Thank you, B.'

He smiled for the first time since Christmas. He'd use the trip to talk to her about selling the boat, pruning their things, and moving elsewhere.

On Valentine's Day, Barbs had five thigh-high clay amphorae filled with compost and spring bulbs delivered. 'Happy Valentine.' She pecked him on the cheek.

'Um... thanks.' The yacht swayed a little when they were placed on the upper deck. 'Ever wonder how much everything on board weighs?'

'Don't be daft,' said Barbs. 'Boats float—and this is a big one.'

Barry woke abruptly that night. Had music disturbed him again? The yacht shuddered and there was a loud whooshing. *What the hell?* He leapt out of bed. As the vessel lurched to starboard, he stumbled. He got up, heart thrumming, and dashed into the corridor towards Barbs' cabin. A two-inch current of water met him. He shivered. 'Barbs?' No reply. 'Barbs?' he cried.

'Barry!'

He pitched on, soaking his pyjama bottoms. *It's freezing.* Inside her room, Barbs was grabbing jewelry and tossing it in a suitcase.

'What the hell are you doing?'

'Rescuing the most important things.'

'We need to go. Now.'

'I'm almost done.' She zipped the suitcase shut. 'Help me.'

'For Christ's sake.' Barry grabbed the suitcase. 'Heavy!'

They waded down the corridor, splashing through icy water, teeth chattering with cold. Clambered awkwardly to the upper deck via slippery stairs. The yacht shuddered and tilted to one side. Barry, struggling to keep upright, let go of the suitcase, which skidded across the deck towards the sinking side. Barbs slid after it, grabbing it as if it were a lifebuoy.

'No,' shouted Barry. He seized the railings on the highest part. 'Barbs! Come here.' As he stretched out his hand, the boat jolted.

Splayed on her back now, Barbs slipped under the railings and dropped down into the sea. The yacht was sinking over her like a headstone.

'Oh god, no.' Barry clambered over the railing and hurled himself into the water, as far as possible from the yacht. An icy sensation pierced him; a powerful current tugged him under. His lungs bursting, he forced himself to swim up through fathoms of freezing sea. He surfaced and trod water, catching his breath, muscles numb with cold.

The Blind Ark had gone under. He looked left and right, but his eyes strained in the dark. *Where the hell's Barbs?*

'Mr Blind!' A torch beam hovered nearby. Three shadowy figures were on the lit jetty, silhouettes of hope. 'Mr Blind. It's Joe Patten.'

Small waves sloshed over him, pushing him away from the jetty. His face and fingers ached with cold.

A life buoy landed near, attached to a rope. 'Grab it,' shouted Joe. 'Swim, man, swim!'

Barry forced his weary muscles to do the breast-stroke. Joe then reeled him and hauled him onto the jetty. 'We need to get you warm, Mr Blind.' Joe whipped off Barry's soaked pyjamas and rubbed his body with a towel.

'Barbs!' Barry's teeth chattered. He lifted one foot, then the other, which burned cold against the concrete.

'Stand on this.' Joe placed a towel on the ground. Barry

obeyed. 'We're searching for Barbs with torches. It's not safe to enter the water. The rescue team will be here any minute.' Joe wrapped Barry in another towel and put a blanket over that.

'Derek,' shouted Joe. 'Come here! Take Barry to *Victoria's Wave*.'

'No! Barbs,' said Barry.

'We'll find her,' said Joe. 'You *must* warm up.'

Barry was faint. 'I…'

A loud shout. Barry swung around. Someone was pointing at the water. 'Oh, god,' they gasped.

Barry staggered to their side. The torch beam illuminated a raft of floating stuff: pink armbands, a blue plastic octopus, a globe, swimming floats, and, in the middle, something larger. Face down. Lifeless.

***

Barry sold the cottage and bought a bungalow close to Anna. He gave away all possessions that weren't essential. An investigation found that *The Blind Ark* sank partly due to a design flaw and partly due to all the weight. 'We're not here to assign blame,' said the coroner, 'but I must say that you are an intelligent man, Mr. Blind, and I cannot understand you and your late wife's complete lack of foresight aboard the yacht.'

Grief and shame caught in Barry's throat as he murmured, 'I can't either.'

He struggled to sleep, and to distract himself from thoughts about Barbs, he spent the nocturnal hours reading books about the natural world—about ancient woodland, seals in the Thames, coastal erosion. Every morning he took Bella, his adopted black Labrador, for a walk, trying to focus on the wispy clouds that floated across the sky, not the dark ones that crowded his heart; attempting to suppress the memory of Barbs's pretty eyes and how she used to touch his hand.

At the bungalow, Radio 4 would play all day to block out his maudlin ruminations. *Why were we so foolish?*

Would she still be here if I'd seen the obvious danger? Without the radio, such questions ricocheted like bullets around his head.

On Mondays, he volunteered at the Citizen's Advice Bureau, something Anna persuaded him to try. He offered financial guidance to people who put him in mind of Skye.

Three days per week, he collected his granddaughters from primary school. Ellie would rush up to him and exclaim, 'Look at my drawing!' or 'Hold my hand, Grandpa.' Rose would approach more quietly, pressing something she'd found into his palm—an autumn leaf, a pebble shaped like a crescent moon. He walked them home, clasping their little hands tightly as if they were the last beings on earth.

THE SHAMAN OF SMOG

From the top of Colina del Este, Esteban glimpsed clouds drifting over the mountain in the distance. His lips parted as he stared. He shifted his gaze eastwards. Just outside of town, flames of burning natural gas shot skywards from metal stacks forty metres high, akin to giant Bunsen burners. The smog, suspended above the town, tinted the atmosphere faint mustard. The cruel sun penetrated through, melting pools of tar like black ice cream in the gutters. The muscles in Esteban's chest tightened, the air seeming to burn him as he inhaled. He undid the top button on his white shirt and stroked his neck with his fingers.

Pain gripped his lungs. He coughed hard for a couple of minutes, covering his mouth with his hand. Afterwards, his breathing felt laboured, and he rubbed his ribcage for comfort. The attacks were getting more frequent. An image from a nightmare came back: trapped in an underground cell, unable to escape.

Damn both Dr. Alonso and Dr. Rivera! Well, he couldn't entirely blame them for following their own medical advice and leaving town, but what was he to do? The nearest proper doctor was now a two-hour journey to the south. And could he afford medics there, anyway?

Esteban walked down to the Plaza del Mercado. The oil refinery brought many new labourers into the town, and the market bustled with stalls selling hot snacks, fruit and vegetables, bread, sweets, folk-healing regalia, and crafts. In the air hung the smell of *churros* and *empanadas*. The market filled much of the plaza, though on one side an old colonial building was supported by steel scaffolding. The regular lines of the scaffolding soothed, while the chaotic marketplace, with its garish colours, disquieted him.

One stall sold folk-healing paraphernalia like herbs, amulets, charms, books of magic, and pictures of saints and healers. He stopped and steepled his fingertips. He was sceptical about traditional healing, although he'd had a soft spot for it as a child. Carmen, his mother's maid, had used it on him. 'This will help, my angel,' she'd say, popping an amulet into his pocket. 'Just don't tell Mummy, okay?'

A Camsa woman in jeans and a tee shirt, with colourful bead bracelets and earrings, was standing behind the stall. 'Good afternoon, Señor Lacunza,' she said.

He tried to place her familiar face.

'I'm Mercedes. Remember? You ran the protests against the refinery. I came to meetings.'

'Ah, yes. That's right. A fat lot of good we did.'

'Are you after something?'

'Herbs perhaps. I have a cough.'

'What kind?'

He pressed a hand to his chest. 'Quite severe and painful. The bouts last minutes.'

'Any other symptoms?'

'Sometimes dizziness and headaches.'

A shadow floated across her eyes and she pointed to a russet powdered herb. 'Maybe... try *cuacia*.'

'You don't sound too convinced.'

'This sickness is tricky to treat.' She leaned forward and murmured, 'It's caused by sorcery.'

His Catholic mother kept amulet bracelets and evil eye talismans hidden under her bed, even though she claimed that sorcery and witchcraft were nonsense. Esteban's passion for books had led him to question both Catholicism and sorcery. He was taut with doubt, and valued rationality as highly as his mother valued the Virgin Mary. This didn't bring the comfort of certainties, although it made him ask pertinent questions. 'The symptoms are because of the smog, surely,' he said.

Her eyes flickered with fear. 'There's evil in this place.'

'What would you suggest I do?'

'Heard of Santiago Hinchoa? By far the best healer in these parts.'

He nodded, and his stomach tensed into a knot. Troubled by his father's heavy drinking and his parents' nightly rows, the seventeen-year-old Esteban used to sneak out of town to visit Santiago's house. Santiago had taken him under his wing, allowing him to observe healing rituals, and eventually remarked, 'You're a smart kid, Esteban. You have a gift. You should train to be a *curandero* like me.'

Despite being intrigued by Santiago and traditional beliefs, Esteban had doubted his faith in folk healing. 'What I really want is to leave town and study at university.'

'Certain things can't be learned from books.'

'But I love books.'

'Be my apprentice and the spirits will guide you.'

Heat had flushed over Esteban. He hated being told what to do. 'You're not my dad. Leave me alone.' With his heart pumping, he had run all the way home.

The next day, when Santiago had come into town to speak with him, they ended up arguing. 'Go away,' Esteban shouted in the heat of the moment. 'Keep your stupid Indian ways.'

Over the years, Esteban had spotted Santiago around town, but they'd never talked. Remembering his own shameful words still made Esteban blush.

He thanked Mercedes and walked on, furrows denting his forehead. Santiago was the only local healer who might be worth trying, but would the man want to see him? Esteban set his jaw in determination. He had no other options.

Sweat popped from his brow as he phoned his wife, Ana, from a public phone box. Thankfully, he was able to leave a message on the answering machine saying he had unexpected errands and wouldn't return to their bookstore until later. She considered folk medicine to be snake oil.

The corrugated-iron shacks of the oil refinery labourers lined Arbol Street. Television aerials clung to the roofs, like monstrous metal spiders. Esteban wondered how hard life was when that was your home.

At the edge of town, a dirt road sliced through the

forest. There were slender palms, wild banana trees, and rosewoods with branches garlanded by strings of pink orchids. About two kilometres further on, Esteban came across an abandoned rusty truck smothered in yellow climbing lilies. He paused to marvel at the sight and quenched his thirst with water from his bottle.

Sweat smeared his shirt by the time he reached the end of the dirt road, turning the white cotton grey in places. This area was inhabited mainly by Camsa peoples, the forest enclosing the dwellings on three sides. Most of the houses were small buildings with mud-plastered walls; one was larger, with a wooden veranda. Esteban's heart thumped with anxiety about seeing Santiago, but biting down on his lip, he ascended some steps.

In a blue-and-white checked shirt, Santiago sat in a chair on the veranda. Although his hair was grey now, he still had those intelligent eyes set in an ovoid face. 'Esteban. This is a surprise.'

He wiped his brow. 'Hello, Don Santiago.'

'You look hot. Can I get you some water or a beer?'

'I'm afraid this isn't a social visit.'

'How can I help you, then?'

'It's... well, about my health.'

Santiago cocked his head to one side. 'I thought you didn't believe in *curanderos*.'

Esteban couldn't work out whether Santiago's tone was serious or playful. 'I still have doubts, but then I doubt most things.' His chin lowered. 'And I'm ashamed of what I said to you all those years ago.'

An attack of coughing seized Esteban. Pain stabbed him like a skewer, causing him to press a palm to his chest. He rubbed his breastbone in a slow, circular manner until the symptoms eased.

The old man's expression became grave. 'You have dizziness and headaches, too?

Esteban nodded.

'This is strong sorcery.'

'It's the smog.'

'I always liked your honesty. We're both right.' He

stood up. 'The sorcery lies *within* the smog; *gringos* are powerful magicians. I can't get the evil out of the air, but I can try to remove it from your lungs.' He beckoned. 'Come in.'

'You're sure?'

'Yes.' The old man still moved with the quiet purpose that Esteban remembered.

He recognised the room, too. Wooden chairs were on one side. On the other, an altar had items like candles, pictures of saints and healers, stones, a toy car, flowers, a doll, figurines of Saint Miguel and José Gregorio Hernández, and a bottle of brandy. Esteban admired the religious ingenuity of taking objects from different cultures and making them holy.

Santiago dragged a chair into the middle of the room. 'Sit.'

Esteban sat.

Santiago disappeared and then returned wearing a cream poncho decorated with dark stripes and a necklace strung with what looked like bone beads. At the altar, Santiago lit candles and copal incense as he whispered prayers.

As Esteban gazed at the man, his heart became a little lighter, a little warmer.

Holding a fan made of leaves and feathers, Santiago approached. Self-conscious, Esteban shifted in the chair. Waving the rustling fan in rhythm with his deep voice, Santiago chanted what appeared to be sounds rather than words. He fell silent, leaned close to Esteban, took a powerful suck of air, turned his head, spat, and resumed singing. A ghostly presence touched Esteban, and he shivered.

Santiago repeated the actions until beads of sweat broke out across his forehead. He shook his head. 'It's no use. We must take *yagé*.'

'We?'

'You, too.'

'I can't. I have a wife and kids now.'

'It's just a healing rite.'

'Is it even safe to take, given my chest?'

'You'll be fine. I'm here. And my apprentice, Pablo, will join us, too.'

Esteban hesitated.

'You know, when you were a lad, you told me about the intense pictures *yagé* gave you. You have a gift, Esteban.'

'I... I'm not sure I believe in it.'

'Belief's irrelevant. The visions come from beyond that. Remember?'

Esteban's memory carried him adrift to the few times he'd tried *yagé* in this room and had intoxicating visions. He looked into the old man's intelligent, lively eyes. For the first time in ages, Esteban's heart pulsed with excitement. 'Yes, I do.'

'Wait here.' Santiago disappeared through a doorway.

What should Esteban do about Ana? There was no way to let her know he'd be much later than expected. Oh well, he was never normally irresponsible. When Santiago didn't return for a while, Esteban went to examine the altar more closely, but then chastised himself for being nosey and returned to his chair.

Eventually, Santiago came in with a thin young man and a bowl of dark liquid. 'This is Pablo,' he said.

The man nodded a greeting and sat.

On the altar, Santiago poured the liquid into cups. He lit more copal incense and called on God, Saint Miguel, and various spirits. He handed a cup to Esteban.

'If I need to puke?'

Santiago pointed to a bucket out on the veranda.

The *yagé* tasted bitter, acrid. For some time, nothing happened, and all three sat in a silence filled with the croaks, trills and hoots of the surrounding forest. Then Esteban's stomach heaved. Rushing out to the veranda, he vomited several times. When the retching stopped, he rinsed his mouth with water and returned inside. His body trembled. It was starting...

In ebbs and flows, in rivulets and waves, the yagé pictures came. Pink floral forms swayed in slow motion;

green lines like forest vines that swelled into emerald snakes. The serpents twisted and turned, curling and swirling through the air. Then dissolved, like an old movie on the screen, flickering, flickering...

Singing intruded into Esteban's awareness, Santiago's voice.

A tall metallic tree materialised, its iron branches jabbing the heavens. From the top, a chimney of fire shot upwards. The heavens screeched, a high-pitched wail. A grinning white monkey with horns climbed the tree, immune to the torrid heat. Smoke drifted across the sky in thick curtains, the world growing sodden with fumes, all dark and ominous...

Esteban sensed a body, a presence, close to him.

Santiago, tall as a tree, held up a fan of iridescent feathers. Santiago, sucking the blackness from the sky, sucking until it vanished. A light glowed and kept growing. Beautiful birds of azure and yellow swooped by. Books materialised in mid-air and opened themselves. Silver writing rolled off the pages, a waterfall of letters tumbling, pooling on the ground, glittering. The luminous waterfall dissolved, quiet darkness descending...

***

Esteban awoke on the veranda. He sat up, rubbing his slightly throbbing head. The pink of dawn haloed the tops of the trees. His watch told him it was 6.30 AM. Christ! He must get back to Ana. He stood up.

Santiago appeared with a glass of water. 'For you.'

The drink eased Esteban's parched throat. 'Thanks.'

'How were the visions?'

'Interesting.'

'You saw the tower of fire.'

'How do you know?'

Santiago gave the merest of shrugs. 'You saw me, too.'

'Yes.'

'How are the lungs?'

Esteban took a few deep breaths. 'Yes, they feel better.'

'Good. The evil seems to have gone, at least for now. Take this to strengthen your lungs. The instructions are on the bottle.' He gave Esteban some herbal tincture, and then gently patted his face. 'It's been good to see you, my friend. Don't leave it so long next time.' He indicated a truck waiting. 'I have to visit another patient now.'

'What do I owe you?'

'Call it eight thousand pesos.'

Esteban handed the money over. 'Can I get a lift into town?'

'Sorry. We're going the other way.' Santiago descended the steps and got into the truck. As the vehicle vanished, an invisible thread that seemed to be tied to bind the two men together tugged at Esteban's heart.

In the forest, the monkey hoots made him grin. When had he last felt this happy? He jogged for a bit, taking gulps of air. Images came back to him from the previous night—emerald snakes and silver writing. He felt alive, as if he were a teenager again, and connected to a mystery beyond—or was that just the aftermath of the hallucinogen?

The healing had worked! He'd always doubted it, considering Santiago to be an astute psychologist and herbalist rather than a man with spiritual powers. Had Esteban lived a life too constrained by reason? Could the indigenous peoples and their *yagé* withstand *gringo* ways after all? He plucked a yellow climbing lily from a tree and inhaled its delicate scent.

On the outskirts of town, he brushed vainly at the dirt stains on his shirt.

At his shop, he halted, summoning the courage to enter. Inside, Ana glowered at him.

'So sorry. I got really drunk with Paulo and completely lost track of time,' he lied.

'I've been worried sick. Why didn't you phone?'

'It won't happen again. Promise.'

'It better not. But look at yourself. Go and shower.'

That day, Esteban smiled warmly at customers, arranged a colourful new display for magical realism titles, and even kissed Ana on the cheek twice. When they closed the shop, he said, 'Let's take the kids to Vivos for a meal tonight.'

'Why?' she asked.

'I'm in the mood to celebrate.'

'Celebrate what?'

He opened his arms wide. 'Life.'

'You should get drunk with Paulo more often.'

***

Three days later, still feeling well, Esteban popped out at lunchtime to buy bread. The smog hung in the air, but he strolled along humming. He stopped, noticing a yellow and green beaded earring on the pavement, one of the indigenous crafts sold in the market. Tar speckled it. He picked the thing up, which resembled a tiny hummingbird, and cradled it in his palm. 'Just chuck it,' Ana's voice said in his mind, but he put it in his bag to clean.

As he neared the bank, pain flickered in his lungs. He tensed; it eased. Near the bakery, a second twinge. He took a slow, deep breath. The pain returned with a vengeance, and he coughed and coughed.

He pressed a palm to his brow, grimacing. Was the *gringo* magic too strong for Santiago? Or had Esteban been deluding himself? He'd been desperate for a cure, but the folk magic hadn't worked, the benefits only a temporary placebo. Wasn't that the truth? Something sour caught in his throat and a heaviness settled into his heart.

What would he say to Santiago if he saw him again? What?

He noticed the flames from the oil refinery outside town, shooting upwards as if burning a hole in the sky. Images from his *yagé* vision flashed before his eyes: a white-horned monkey in the fire and the world soaked in fumes. He gasped as sudden, deep knowledge came to him, the kind Santiago would call intuition.

It isn't just my life vanishing into that hole. All life is.

Calmer Karma

A wolf's eyes normally gleam cold and sharp like a metallic moon, but Killer's eyes reflected the open sky.

'You're a wolf, Killer,' said Volverang, leader of the Belzamine wolf pack.

'So?'

Volverang pricked his ears. 'So you're a carnivore incarnate and woodland assassin. That doesn't square with being a Buddhist.'

Killer met the dominant wolf's gaze. 'But I no longer crave violence. I want to be compassionate. I seek to pierce the heart of existence.'

'You should be more concerned with piercing the heart of a rabbit,' said Volverang, spittle dribbling from the corner of his mouth. 'You were my protégé, the cruellest, most cunning wolf of all. But now, because of this Buddhist whatchamacallit, you're causing consternation in the pack. Some young wolves are even asking questions. We wolves hunt, feed, have sex, and sleep. We don't ask questions, nor do we waffle on about existence.'

Killer cocked his head to the side, saying nothing.

Volverang picked at some rabbit fluff caught around his claw. 'How did you learn about this Buddhist crap, anyway?'

'From a human hermit who lives by the river. One day I went hunting, hoping to eat his chickens, but somehow, mysteriously, we ended up in a long conversation about Buddhism. He made me see the error of my ways. That's when I changed. I now follow a path of kindness.'

Volverang gestured with a paw to a route through the forest. 'You can follow that path, too, which takes you well away from here. We lupines are loyal to our kind, not to kindness.' He snorted and a bubble of snot protruded from one nostril.

'You're saying…?'

'I'm banishing you.'

Killer swallowed. 'So be it.'

Killer slipped into the forest, strolling quickly. After putting some distance between him and the wolf pack, he stopped to practise the meditation he'd learned from the human. Pure awareness of the 'now' was the essence of Buddhism. He was mindful of the Scots pines stretching skywards, their bark powdered an orangey hue; the arias of blackbirds; the heady scent of hawthorn; and the soft wind nuzzling his fur.

Killer wandered on. He didn't miss the pack with their carnivorous ways. The trees were sufficient companions, and in the gentle breeze, their branches seemed to sigh, as if murmuring their approval of him.

The forest segued to a grassy meadow in which a group of greyish-brown rabbits grazed. The sun bathed them in clear light. *Aha.* Here was a chance to atone for all the times he'd devoured such harmless creatures without a thought. In his life as Killer-the-Cruel, he'd surely notched up enough bad karma to be reincarnated as, at best, a tapeworm. As Killer strolled towards the rabbits, he was surprised they didn't back away. Nor did their eyes glaze over with the black enamel of fear. Instead, they sat up, ears pricked, studying him.

Killer lowered his muzzle. 'Good day, rabbits. I know I'm a wolf, the scourge of your kind. But recently I've also become a Buddhist. I've come to make it up to you, to apologise profusely if I've ever eaten any of your, er, relatives.'

The rabbits hopped closer, with expressions familiar to a wolf. One rabbit spoke: 'We got fed up with being eaten, so we've changed, too. We're no longer fluffy pacifists. We've become partial to orgiastic outbreaks of violence.'

Another rabbit snarled, 'So be afraid, wolf.'

The rabbits encircled him. The last thing he saw was a militia of fur and floppy ears advancing, muttering, 'Kill him, kill him.'

Family, Fungi, Friends

I was gobsmacked when Mum told us that the daughter of Hugo Speedwell, the local Member of Parliament, had booked to come to our eco-commune on an 'experience week'. 'What? After he called us "crusty tree huggers who should get proper jobs" on television?' I said.

'It's odd.' Mum was chopping a home-grown squash at the kitchen table.

'You think she's coming to snoop?' I was cutting carrots at the table too.

'It's possible.'

'But we've got nothing to hide.' Tuft, my older brother, stood by the door. He glanced in the wall mirror, using two fingers to spruce up his dyed-blond quiff.

'Since when did that matter?' said Mum. 'Remember Hugo Speedwell claimed our compost toilets aren't sanitary and our mushroom packaging looks filthy?'

'He's an idiot. Doesn't believe the climate crisis is real.' I sliced through a carrot.

Dark bags underscored Mum's eyes. 'But he's powerful. And you've heard the rumours about Mr Biggermort.'

'Yes.' Our six-year-old eco-commune in rural Wales rented land and two factory buildings from a rich landowner, Mr Biggermort, who was apparently considering refusing the extension to our lease when it came up for renewal next year. Hugo Speedwell wasn't the only local unhappy with an eco-commune on their doorstep.

'Anyway, I'd like *you* to mentor the girl, Chan,' said Mum.

'Why does Chan always get the interesting jobs?' moaned Tuft.

Mum shot him a "drop the attitude" look. We all knew he would hit on Pia if she was pretty. Mum's gaze settled on me. 'Would you? Get to know her a bit while you're mentoring her and see if you can suss what her real intentions are.'

'Sure.' I scooped the cut carrots into a bowl. 'She might just be a youngster into eco stuff.'

'True, but go easy on the environmental rants around her anyway, okay?' said Mum.

'I'll try my best.' Though I was pleased to be trusted in this way at nineteen, a shrinking feeling settled around my heart. I couldn't bear the idea of Rootiful, my home, being closed down. I had spent much of my teenage life here and Mum, a founder, had put her life savings into making it a success.

The "experience week" began on a sunny morning. The volunteers assembled for an orientation talk near the tents they slept in. Pia, the politician's daughter, stuck out, dressed daftly as she was in a lilac dress, gold jewellery and heeled purple sandals. The others, all in jeans and trainers, were the usual kinds who attended—university students, hipsters, ecologists.

Mum allocated a job and a Rootiful mentor to each volunteer.

I approached Pia. 'I'm Chan. I'm mentoring you.'

'Pia.' Tall and willowy, she peered down her equine nostrils. The subtle scent of citrusy perfume clung to her.

'Looking forward to the week?'

'Mm.' She twiddled her gold bracelet.

'I take it you're into eco stuff,' I said to test the waters.

Her gaze drifted to the distance. 'So, where's this factory, then?'

Pia wasn't interested in chatting, so I accompanied her silently across our fifty-acre field. It was hedged by oak trees on three sides; the wooden eco homes we had built clustered on one side, near the stream, and the factory buildings were on the other. The sun warmed my face; the clouds threw shadowy shapes across the lush Welsh hills in the distance. As Pia surveyed the field with a suspicious frown, unease coursed through me.

The factory, which had a distinct musty odour, was a warehouse divided into work and storage rooms. I introduced Pia to several Rootiful coworkers. They all smiled hello, but she gave them the merest of nods. I showed her some mycelium panels, which were speckled with blends of oat, wheat and acorn colours. 'This is what we are known for. Mycelium material is strong. You can mould it to any shape, and it's used in packaging and in construction. Eco-friendly and doing well commercially.'

Pia tugged her dark-blonde plait over her shoulder, twiddling its end.

I spent the morning showing her the ropes. 'This room is where we add the mycelium blend to bio-waste and place it within the moulds... In this room, the mix develops... And look! In just weeks, it's grown to form a firm block, filled with fibres that act like glue.'

Pia said little but kept running her querying gaze around whatever room we were in, which put me on edge. The "she's snooping" theory edged up a notch.

At lunchtime, Pia said she would go to her tent.

'You don't want lunch?'

'Not today. Can I get a phone signal here?'

'We don't use mobiles and suggest visitors put theirs aside.'

She shrugged.

'Well, other visitors say you can get a signal if you walk halfway up that.' I pointed to a hill a fair hike away, meaning it would take effort for her to send texts.

We enjoyed communal lunches in the pavilion here, a large building made of a wooden frame and mycelium panels. I joined the queue and was handed a steaming plate of lentil stew with homemade brown bread.

Tuft was already at a table. With his sea-green eyes lined in black kohl, baggy grey linen shirt and thong necklace, he resembled an underweight indie singer. 'No Pia?' he asked.

'No.' I told him where she was.

'Maybe she needs time to herself. This place can be, like, full on.'

After lunch, I found Pia hunched outside her tent, writing in a notebook. 'I came to collect you.'

She snapped the book shut. 'Is it time already?'

On the afternoon shift, I showed Pia how to pop the

mycelium products out of the moulds—my favourite bit. They would then be heat-treated to stop them growing. The first time she tried, she cracked the product. 'Oops,' she said, without looking guilty.

'Careful. Try again.'

She managed to crack two more before she mastered the technique. She then worked hard, but said little.

I told her that after dinner, a group of us were going to build a bonfire and have some wine and a singsong. We were doing it for our guests. 'You'll come?'

'No.'

'It'll be fun. We could hang out and chat.'

'Early night for me.' She frowned down at her dress, which had picked up plenty of factory dirt.

That evening, a full moon perched brightly above. The woody bonfire smell filled the air; its flames crackled. After we'd had a few drinks, a couple of friends played the djembe drums while Tuft strummed his guitar. I was pleased he was here. He wasn't as committed as me to Rootiful and in the evenings often took off to the nearby town to practise with his band.

Everyone joined in singing until Angie, a curvy guest with aquamarine eyes, asked to borrow the guitar. She played Taylor Swift songs, singing along in a pitch-perfect voice.

Afterwards, I told Angie how good she was.

'Aren't you the one who's working with Pia?'

'Yes.'

'I was stunned when I found out her dad's the Tory MP.'

'She seems different from most of you who come.'

'Stuck up, you mean? Bloody Tories.' Angie pressed a palm to her mouth. 'Sorry. Shouldn't swear.'

A hand touched my arm—Tuft's. 'I'm heading home. Coming?' he said.

'Sure.'

'Walk with us?' he said to Angie.

'I've promised to play another song. Another time, you can walk me back to my tent.' She smiled flirtatiously.

'You're on.' He grinned.

Tuft and I wandered off. 'You didn't have band practice tonight?' I asked.

'Decided to join in here instead. Thought you'd be pleased.'

'You mean you wanted to check out the women?'

'What? Are you Mum now?'

'Who do you fancy then? Angie?'

'She's quite cute.'

I lit my torch and we meandered through a small wood, the smell of moss floating on the darkness. As we came out of the trees, Tuft pointed at someone sitting on a tree stump ahead. 'Who's that?'

I cleared my throat as we got closer, and Pia turned around. 'Hi,' I said. 'You okay?'

'I'm watching the stars.'

'I think Venus and Jupiter are, like, visible tonight,' said Tuft.

'They are there and there,' she said.

I followed her pointing finger.

'You know about stars?' said Tuft.

'A little. I've got a place to study astrophysics at uni this September.'

'Really?' I said, surprised.

'Brainy, huh?' Tuft's smile was feral.

'This is Tuft, my brother,' I said.

'I see the resemblance. Same eyes and physique,' she said.

'I'd love to go to uni too,' said Tuft.

'To study what?' Pia asked.

'Music production.'

'Oh.'

'How are you finding it here?' asked Tuft.

'It's okay.'

'Nice to hear someone gush.' Tuft grinned. 'Walk back with us?

As we strolled along, Tuft said, 'I bet most astrophysics students aren't as hot as you.'

'So?' she said curtly.

'Do you, like, have a boyfriend?'

'How do you know I'm even straight?'

He smiled. 'My gaydar has never failed me yet.'

'Leave her be, Tuft,' I said.

She gave me a piercing glance. 'I don't need rescuing.'

After we dropped her off at her tent, he said, 'Shame she's prickly because she's, like, easy on the eye.' He twiddled his wristband. 'You're right not to trust her.'

The following day at work, I left Pia to check the developing mixes in their moulds and skipped off to what was supposed to be a long meeting, but when it was cancelled, I returned straight away. Pia wasn't at her work station. I found her in an adjacent storeroom taking photos on her phone of shelves of mycelium panels. I cleared my throat.

Her cheeks flushed rosehip pink. She shoved her phone in her bag, which she had with her. Her notebook, lying open on a shelf, a pen by it, was swept into the bag, too.

I frowned. 'Why are you photographing in here?'

'No reason. Well, I like the look of the panels.'

'What?'

'I, er, find the colours interesting. Sorry. I'll get back to work.' She slunk back to the other room and started checking on the mixes. An awkward silence ensued until she asked, 'Do you enjoy working here, Chan?'

'Yes.'

'You don't want to go to university like your brother?'

'What's the point of getting 30k in debt and reading Shakespeare or whatever when the planet is in so much danger?'

'Do you really believe that?'

'Didn't you read the latest UN report?' I gestured around the room. 'If humans have a future, places like this are it.'

'But surely any studying has value.'

I was getting het up so I took a breath, calming myself. 'Well, we have a study day regularly here.'

'Studying what?'

'The science of fungi at the moment. It's not astrophysics, but fungi are so cool.'

'In what way?'

'Did you know the largest living organism is a fungus, the Armillaria ostoyae, which covers 10 square kilometres.'

'No, I didn't.'

That evening, I filled Mum in on Pia's antics. 'She acted guiltily. Something didn't add up.'

A squint of worry crossed Mum's brow. 'Hmm. Her dad did claim on television that our panels look really unhygienic and grubby.'

'I've seen her writing in that notebook before.'

'And you have no sense yet of why she's come here?'

'No. She's hard work to talk to.'

An ugly pinch formed in Mum's brow as she pondered.

I wanted to be more useful to Mum. 'Maybe I could take a quick look in the notebook if the opportunity arises.'

'I'm not sure that's ethical.' She let out a breath. 'Do you know that Rootiful got an anonymous hate letter today, postmarked locally? It said we weren't welcome here and our time was nearly up.'

'What?' I exclaimed in shock. Though we sometimes got mean remarks in town, we hadn't had that before. 'Do you reckon it's somehow connected to Pia being here?'

'I just don't know.'

'Why don't I try to sneak a quick peek at her notebook? I won't read it all. Just get a brief sense of what she's writing about Rootiful.'

'Well, alright then.'

Two days later, Pia and I were filling moulds at work when she let out a gasp.

'Are you okay?' I asked.

She grimaced, as if in pain.

'Can I get you anything?'

'My bag, please,' she whispered. 'From over there.'

I retrieved it from a shelf. She removed her work gloves and retrieved some pills and a flask of water. She gulped two pills down, then inhaled and pressed her palms to her thighs.

'Period pain?'

'No. The painkillers will take fifteen minutes to kick in. Mind if I have a break?'

'Sure. There's a bench under the tree outside. Sit there?'

When she had gone, I used the opportunity to search her bag. No notebook inside. *Damn*. Her phone *was* there and I was tempted for a moment to take it out and switch it on to see if I could access her photos. But it was pointless as she surely had a passcode. A noise outside in the corridor startled me, so I guiltily closed the bag.

On the way home, I asked, 'What was wrong with you earlier, if you don't mind me asking?'

'It's a chronic problem I've had for a few years, just something I have to live with.'

'You looked in pain. Does it happen often?'

Her gaze shifted quickly towards the hills. 'I don't want to bore you.'

On impulse, I invited her for dinner and was surprised that she agreed.

On the barbecue behind our house, the peppers and courgettes, doused in oil and oregano, exuded an aromatic fragrance as they cooked. I tended to them, and a few friends sat on the ground, chatting about veganism with Angie and another volunteer. Pia sat alone to one side.

'Are you vegan, Pia?' asked Angie.

'No,' said Pia.

'That figures.'

'Meaning?' Pia stared at Angie as she wrapped her arms around her knees.

'Come on. Let's eat,' I said to deflect from the tension.

'Did someone say food's up?' Tuft swaggered out of the house's back door, holding an open bottle of wine. Dressed in baggy jeans and a Radiohead t-shirt. 'Anyone want wine?'

'Me please,' said Pia.

I served the food and Tuft poured glasses of wine. He then sat next to Pia for the meal and they became involved in conversation.

The following day, Pia made more effort to talk to me. She asked me about the tattoo on my biceps.

'It's a chanterelle mushroom.' I held up my arm to show her. 'My namesake. I'm Chanterelle.'

'Cool name.'

'Have you got any tattoos?'

'One only.' She showed me a tiny clam shell on the side of her neck.

'Nice. Does it have any meaning?'

She hesitated before speaking. 'When I was a child, we used to go to the seaside in Cornwall every Easter and I collected all the shells I could. I loved their shapes and how they once protected living beings. I took them all home and arranged them just so around my bedroom. At that age, I believed they were protecting me. Stupid, I know.'

'Doesn't sound stupid to me.' I wondered why she needed protection when young, and her comments made me wonder if I had her pegged correctly. She was clearly sensitive, although that wouldn't stop her from being a snoop. We chatted more, and the conversation was so easy that I forgot I was meant to be observing her.

A day later, as we were preparing mycelium mix, I decided to ask about her father. 'Your dad's a Tory politician, isn't he?'

'Yes.'

'What is his opinion of you being here?'

She avoided my eyes. 'Not sure.'

'It's just I've heard he isn't keen on this place.'

'Should I be concerned when this is uneven in texture?' She presented some mycelium mix to me on her palms, clearly altering the subject.

Later that day, I bumped into Angie. 'I reckon I should tell you,' she said. 'I wandered into the empty pavilion earlier and found Pia filming its mycelium walls with her phone. I asked what she was up to and she got all flustered. It crossed my mind that she's here on a mission for her dad.'

'Oh?' My suspicions about Pia spiked.

On study day, Ellen, a leader, taught us more about the Wood Wide Web. 'There's an underground web of roots and fungi which connects trees to one another and allows them to communicate.' The class lasted hours. Afterwards, as I walked home with Pia, she said, 'You were right. Fungi *is* fascinating.'

'If you study astrophysics, where will that lead?'

She pointed up. 'The stars.'

'That's *my* favourite part of our skyline.' I indicated a hill in the distance.

'Looks like a good viewpoint.'

'The other volunteers are going up there on Sunday. You should walk with them.' I felt bad that I was trying to get her out of the way to read her notebook.

'I'd rather eat a cowpat.'

'Pardon?'

'I don't get on with Angie.'

The day before Pia was due to leave, I told her, 'Tuft and I are going to the pub in the valley later. Fancy coming?'

'Love to.'

My conscience twinged because it was a ruse. We would go together and I would return alone early, feigning a stomachache, to search in her tent for the notebook.

Pia wore makeup and a slinky grey dress; her hair fell loosely down her shoulders.

'You brush up well.' Tuft smiled.

'Thanks.' Her cheeks pinkened.

At the pub, we bought drinks. When Pia visited the toilet, I said, 'When she returns, I'm going to make my excuses. Keep her here, okay?' I didn't think it'd be hard as they fancied each other.

I jogged the mile back and snuck into Pia's tent with a torch. After five minutes of scrabbling around, my palms sweating, I found the notebook hidden under her pillow. I sat on the bed, hesitating through guilt before reassuring myself I was doing this for Rootiful's sake. The first page looked like a diary entry:

I was unsure about coming to the commune, but anything's better than all that summer hols time chez moi. It's a little Dullsville here. No Nexstar telescope or Netflix. They're so proud of their stupid mycelium, too. It makes me a bit sad for them.

Irritation shot through me. I flicked quickly through a few pages and then read:

My initial impression was that Chan was a rustic yokel, but actually she's cool and alert to the world and its marvels. Refreshingly different from my social media obsessed classmates. I'm finding the people here nicer than I expected. Zero snarky comments (apart from an occasional dart from Angie-the-Banshee).

I scrolled on, stopping at:

Chan's brother, Tuft. Just pronouncing his name slips air over your lips. Luscious Tuft, with his sexy eyes the green of sea glass.

A few pages further:

My pain was bad today. Chan helped me out. Even asked what was wrong with me. I welled up. What a dope! But nobody asks about my pain at home, as if it's a grubby little secret to be buried in a box. Certainly, the King of the Bastards never asks. He resents it because my having fibromyalgia is a 'personal weakness', apparently! I hate him.

I'm ashamed to admit it, but I came to Rootiful to embarrass him because he cares so much about his stupid political reputation. He was livid when I told him. Shouted that I was embarrassing him. Tough shit, you bastard.

I didn't expect to really like it here, but I'm surprised at how caring the community seems and how it has prompted me to reflect far more on our relationship to the environment. Even fungi is growing on me (not literally, obvs). It's beautiful to behold and using it makes sense in eco terms. I keep wanting to photograph the mycelium panels. How geeky!

Guilt stabbing at me, I closed the notebook. Pia was no snoop, just an unhappy girl spilling her heart.

Back home, I filled Mum and Tuft briefly in without giving away too many of Pia's secrets.

'It's a relief,' said Mum. 'We clearly misread things. I feel terrible we invaded her privacy now.'

On the day Pia left, I was still feeling guilty.

Tuft grinned as she kissed him on the cheek. 'Come back and visit us soon,' he said.

'I might do that.' Pia gestured to the pavilion. 'I'm aware there's uncertainty about Rootiful's future. If it'll help, I'm willing to talk to Mr Biggermort or the press to vouch for how professional and kind you all are.'

'Wow. That's generous. Thanks.' An unexpected wave of affection hit me, knowing that could get her into trouble with her father.

'Thanks for being a super cool host.' She hugged me and stepped back, looking like she was determined not to cry.

BUTTERFLIES AND A GUN

Butterflies plagued Wessely's stomach. He was at the top of Bedlan Hill, heading toward the city centre for the showdown with Leon Monokov. Above, the sun hid timidly behind bloated grey clouds. To his right were a pawnbroker and Poundland shop, not the deli and bookshop that had stood there a year ago.

A grey-haired woman, carrying a vase of buddleia sprigs in one hand, stopped in front of him. As the pavement had narrowed, Wessely was forced to halt, too.

Staring at his midriff, she said, 'You have butterflies.'

Several butterflies *were* fluttering by his gut. He flicked at one, but his hand missed it and brushed his belly.

'Careful. That's a rare Giant Swallowtail.' She proffered a business card: *Felicity Stone, Psycholepidopterist*. 'I do consultations, you know.'

Wessely frowned, wondering if he should step into the road to get past her.

'A psycholepidopterist is someone who interprets butterflies in people's guts,' she said.

'I don't believe in that sort of thing.'

'A sceptic, eh?' The woman levelled her eyes at his belly. 'Well, two Dingy Skippers fluttering like that suggest considerable anxiety. A Swallowtail shows you're a good person by nature. Hang on...' Surprise registered on her face. 'A Silver-Studded Blue near your hip. Have you got a gun?'

He baulked. 'I'm afraid that's none of your business.'

'Please don't go looking for trouble.'

'Isn't life trouble by definition?'

'Here, let me.' She put away her business card and pulled a sprig of buddleia from the vase. The butterflies were drawn onto it.

Wessely's stomach relaxed. 'Um, thanks.'

'Please don't use the gun or you'll regret it.' She nodded a curt goodbye before she walked off, taking the butterflies with her.

Should he listen? Wessely knew his mind was frazzled; he hadn't slept well for months. He pressed his hand to his jacket pocket, feeling the semi-automatic pistol inside. *Do I even have it in me to use it?* Then Leon Monokov flew to mind again, the man whose signature was on all those letters. Wessely's jaw tightened in determination and he strode off down Bedlan Hill.

Guns weren't something he'd ever thought about until two months ago. His four closest friends—two couples—had gifted him this one shortly before they'd fled the city. 'Just in case you ever need it,' Jed said. Wessely stared at the thing, unable to reply, in shock anyway because his friends had confessed they'd sold their flats—for a pittance—and bought a tiny property together three hundred kilometres away, where the country was a little less chaotic and dangerous. 'Sorry to spring this on you, but we have to think of Hatty and Bella.' Their ten-year-old daughters had recently witnessed three of their teachers fatally shot.

It stung that Wessely's friends hadn't broached the idea of him going, too. Here he was today about to use their pistol.

When he got to Mudslide Road, his nerves were fizzing. The doorways were chock-a-block with the homeless. A poster declared, 'The Temple of Oracular Octopuses Invites You to Discover Your Destiny'; strange cults had proliferated during the Time of Chaos. *The plural octopi is preferable to octopuses, but both are technically correct.* He knew this because he was—well, had been, until his unceremonious firing three months ago—a copywriter.

The memory of his manager telling him he was being let go flashed like a lighthouse beacon.

'But I've worked here for fifteen years.' Wessely remembered his state of disbelief. 'I'll never get another job. Not right now.'

The manager told him there was a loophole in the contract for unprecedented situations such as now—the Time of Chaos.

A noise burst the bubble of his memory. An armoured police van rattled past, siren blaring. He hurried on, thinking once more of Leon Monokov.

Goldacre Street in the Financial District was bustling. Halfway down, a neoclassical building contained the brute that was Morgove Bank. Wessely checked his watch—about half an hour until the meeting. He'd kill time on the stone steps in front of Tesco's Deity Emporium on the opposite side.

Sinking down on the steps, he held his head in his hands. Up to the Time of Chaos, life had never been easy. He hadn't made many friends at school or university despite being a keen student; and much later, his heart had been broken by Marc, his ex-fiancé, a stylish man who'd loved salsa dancing and Wessely's devotion to him more than Wessely himself. But even Marc leaving him for Pablo, the salsa teacher with the liquid hips, had been what Wessely now grasped as ordinary suffering. He'd still had his close friends, a place to live, and money. It hadn't tested him to the breaking point like this.

'We meet again.'

He glanced up to see the woman from earlier, still carrying a vase of buddleia, which had lost its butterflies. *Please go away.*

'You look lost,' she said.

'I know this is Goldacre Street.'

'Not that sort of lost.' She sat next to him, setting the vase down on the steps.

He shifted his seat away, wondering what she wanted this time.

'Do you need to talk?' she said.

'I'm fine,' he said brusquely.

She pointed to the pale-brown butterfly near his gut. 'Really?'

He sighed. 'If I talk, it'll just be one long moan.'

'If you can't moan to a stranger, who can you moan to?'

He noticed her shrewd eyes behind oversized glasses.

She held out her hand. 'I'm Felicity.'

'Wessely.' Her handshake was firm. It seemed odd for a stranger to care. The look of concern on her face prompted him to speak. 'I lost my job three months back and now those sods, please excuse my language,' he gestured towards Morgove Bank, 'are going to repossess my flat.'

'My friend had serious problems with that bank, too.'

He'd applied for so many jobs recently but so had the hundreds of thousands of other unemployed people. At thirty-nine and with no dependents, Wessely was far from first in line. 'I'd been paying my mortgage for eighteen years. Eighteen!' He'd tried to sell the flat too, but the housing market's collapse just after his friends left made that impossible. He adored the flat, anyway. Glancing at his watch, he said, 'My final showdown is in twenty-five minutes.'

'Oh,' she said, frowning. 'Any contingency plans?'

He'd contacted the city council, who'd offered zero help, and it was pointless to turn to his family. His father, an abusive man brimming with barely concealed anger, lived on the other side of the country. Wessely had moved here to get away from him. His mum, a gentle soul who'd played in a jazz band and kept African grey parrots, died of cancer when he was just twenty-one. He still thought about her often.

'Anyone who'd put you up for a bit?' continued Felicity.

His mind darted to the ones who had left, already crammed into a tiny cottage many miles away. He missed them, especially the kids, Bella and Hatty, whom he used to babysit. 'Most people are struggling themselves, aren't they?'

She nodded. 'Too much.'

Wessely's thoughts went to his sanctuary, the flat with his huge jazz collection on vinyl and patterned Turkoman rugs. 'My flat has this little balcony overlooking Redburch Square, where I grow tomatoes, runner beans, sweet peas, petunias...' He felt himself welling up. He'd never imagined himself ending up on the streets. He pushed the grief back. 'Mind if I ask a question?'

'Sure.'

'It's a big question.'

'No guarantee I'll understand it, then.'

'Do you think things happen for a reason?'

'If you're looking for religious insight, this isn't the place.' Felicity gestured over her shoulder to Tesco's Deity Emporium.

'Just after I lost my job, I read this book my manager gave me which said all the bad things that happen are ultimately down to karma and a negative attitude.'

'What rubbish,' she said. 'I hate those Nirvana-for-halfwits books. Given how many are in the same boat, this isn't on you.'

Although rationally he knew she was right, a voice inside still demanded where *he* had gone wrong.

'That doesn't mean you don't have some responsibility for your actions or choices,' she added.

'Even if my choices are complete rubbish?'

'Even then.' Felicity opened her wallet, found a business card, and handed it to him. *Gaiatrope Allotment Initiative* was printed on it, with an address and phone number.

'You like your business cards, don't you?' he said.

'This one isn't mine. Do you know about this place?'

'Sort of.' It was some homeless initiative run by a charity, which took over abandoned blocks in the city and converted their gardens into allotments. 'The people work the gardens, don't they?'

'Yes, they grow fruit and vegetables and make products like jam for sale.'

Hadn't he read articles exposing long working hours and pressure to attend services dedicated to some earth goddess? He couldn't recall properly. Was this woman part of that set-up or sect? He eyed her more suspiciously. 'You give out their cards often, then?'

'Only when someone needs a lifeline.'

Was what he'd taken as her kindness and concern,

really a canny ability to home in on someone vulnerable? It was hard to trust anyone these days.

'The Initiative will try to help you.'

Doubts lingered. He slipped the card into his pocket, anyway. It nestled beside the pistol.

'It's surely better than the streets, and as you sound educated, they might find you an admin role.'

He glanced at his watch. Nearly time.

'Have you already had dealings with the bank official you're meeting?' she asked.

'A little.' Leon Monokov had taken over managing the mortgage three years before, and while Wessely hadn't met the man in person, he'd recognised the photo on the website. A year prior, they'd matched on a dating site and gone for a drink. It was Wessely's first date after his fiancé left. He'd thought it was going well—they chatted easily about their love of jazz—until Leon stood abruptly after a mere hour, with, 'You seem nice, but I'm off. I probably won't contact you again.' Wessely told himself it was the man's prerogative, though the brush-off could have been gentler. Today, that man was going to regret being a dick.

'I don't like the look of that Silver-Studded Blue.' Felicity's gaze was on a butterfly fluttering near him. 'Please don't use the gun, Wessely, if that's your intention.'

He got up abruptly. 'Sorry. Time to go.'

'But—'

'Goodbye.'

As he crossed the road, all his muscles tensed. He clearly looked harmless because the bank's security guard merely asked for his ID card and then waved him inside.

In the waiting room, Wessely sat and dipped his hand in his pocket. Felt the gun. Realised his pits were dripping. He bit down on his lip. If Leon Monokov wouldn't give him an extension, Wessely *had* to do it. He'd rehearsed the scenario while unable to sleep. He'd taken out the unloaded pistol from a bedside drawer, aimed it at the ceiling light, conjuring Leon Monokov to mind, and pulled the trigger. The first few times, he'd felt sick with self-disgust, but then it got easier. He wouldn't kill, anyway—just maim. A shot to the arm or leg. Punishment for the hell Wessely was going through. Legitimate punishment. Leon would get a few days in hospital, and Wessely a few years in jail. At least there was a bed and food there.

Now Wessely was here, his mind reeled. Was Felicity right about choices? If he shot Leon, who did that make him? An unhinged man out of options or simply another thug? If the system was stacked against you, did that justify violence? He'd always considered himself a good person... until now.

'Wessely Browning to room nine,' was announced.

The air seemed to be sucked out of the corridor as he walked. The door echoed when he knocked.

'Come in.'

He shut the door behind him. His mind took the liberty of projecting what the office would look like splattered with the man's blood.

'Mr Browning?' If Leon Monokov recognised Wessely, it didn't register on his face. Leon looked more tired than Wessely remembered, though the aerodynamic features—sharp nose, angular cheekbones—were familiar. 'Please sit.'

Wessely did so.

Leon turned to his computer. 'Um... 24D Alston Heights. Oh... oh dear. Due for repossession on the 24th, I see.' His eyes locked on Wessely. 'I hope you've come to tell me of a change of circumstances.'

A twinge of despair. 'No. I came to see if you'd give me more time.'

Pity flashed in Leon's eyes. 'You're not bringing me any new information. No new job offer?'

'No.'

'Then I'm afraid this meeting has been a waste of time for both of us.'

'But it's so unfair!' Wessely felt the heat rising in his

body. 'I've paid off a huge chunk of the mortgage. You can't steal the flat in my hour of need. You can't.'

'I'm afraid I don't make the rules, Mr Browning.'

'But I've been your customer for eighteen years.'

'Sorry,' Leon said quietly.

Fingering the pistol in his pocket, Wessely tasted acid bile in his throat. 'We've met before, haven't we?'

Leon's eyes showed surprise. 'I thought this was our first meeting in person.'

'I don't mean at the bank. We went on a date about four years ago.'

Leon's cheeks flushed. 'Oh?' He frowned. 'Well, I do recall... vaguely. I went on a lot of dates then.'

As Wessely steeled himself to pull out the gun, Leon's eyes darted to a framed photo on his desk: him hugging an angular-cheeked girl—the spitting image of the man. She must have been about ten, the same age as Bella and Hatty. Seeing the photo threw Wessely completely. 'That's... your daughter?'

'Yes.'

Wessely was sure Leon hadn't mentioned a child on the date.

'Did I leave our date abruptly, by any chance?' asked Leon.

'Very abruptly.'

'Sorry. I was a single parent and was always scooting off to pick up Annabel. I found it hard to be honest about that on first dates. Because of her, I was cautious about arranging second dates, too. Usually decided not to.'

It'd never occurred to Wessely that Leon was thinking about a child.

'Hope you didn't take it personally,' Leon said.

'That kind of thing is easy to take personally.'

Leon's gaze settled on Wessely's pocket, as if wondering what Wessely was doing with his hand. Leon's eyes then flicked up, registering fear, and two Swallowtail butterflies materialised by his chest.

A clear realisation came to Wessely: no way could he shoot this dad.

Next to the pistol was the card Felicity had given him. He pulled that from his pocket instead. 'Look,' he said, and forced himself to ad-lib: 'I *have* applied for a job at this place. On the phone, they said I had a good chance. Give me just one more month in my flat?' A lie, but at least it gave him time to check out the allotment initiative. He did love gardening.

Leon squinted at the card.

'Please?'

Leon let out a breath. 'As you've been an exemplary client for years, I could invoke a little-known clause, which lets me move the bailiff date back by a month. I'll need something concrete from you soon, though. No more excuses.'

A month's reprise? Not much, but relief sizzled through him. Wessely wondered if Leon's guilt over upsetting him four years ago had helped him today.

Outside, the sun cast long shadows on the stone steps. Despair still pressed at the edges of Wessely's mind, but his heart lilted upward, too. He felt proud of himself. He'd made it through the meeting, won time, and shot no-one. The butterflies had gone, too.

He took out the card for the Gaiatrope Allotment Initiative and read the address. His next point of call.

Everything Sucks

Aidan was perched on the ridge of his roof. His legs were straddled on either side, gripping the slate tiles with his knees. His sun lounger was in the garden, but a dark cloud, which reminded him of a wispy spaceship, hovered above. No way was a cloud going to spoil a rare Saturday off from work. Next to him sat his new vacuum cleaner, an EsoTecknic *EverythingSucks* one that had arrived two days ago, made by some hi-tech Chinese company. He'd just hauled it up to the roof via a ladder and secured it with a rope looped around the vacuum's body and tied to the chimney.

Aidan reached for the long black hose of *EverythingSucks*, being careful not to slip off the roof as he picked it up and aimed the nozzle skywards. He glanced right and left, ensuring no one was in the adjacent gardens. What would happen? Perhaps nothing. Perhaps he'd read too much into the instruction manual. He switched the vacuum cleaner onto Extrapower, its second-highest suction.

The cloud that spoiled the pristine sky rushed towards the vacuum cleaner and with a shudder and a schwoop sound, disappeared up the nozzle. *EverythingSucks* trembled. Aidan wobbled too, but steadied himself. He switched the machine off and looked up, his breath quickening. The sky was clear. As the sun warmed his face, he tipped his head back and laughed.

Later, a sunburned Aidan lounged on the sofa, flicking through the 302-page manual for *EverythingSucks*. Part 1 said that if plugged into a socket overnight, "the machine's battery would store enough electricity for four hours of unplugged use"; and the latest lithoquark technology meant the machine could hoover up "dust *and* objects". Aidan had no clue what lithoquark technology was, but who cared? The vacuum cleaner worked brilliantly.

He slipped an arm around *EverythingSucks*, next to him on the sofa, and stretched out his legs. He stroked the vacuum's smooth blue surface, the first thing he'd cuddled for ages, apart from Kipper, his parents' soppy spaniel, whom he dog-sat regularly. On the mantelpiece sat a framed photo of Aidan cuddling Kipper, the pet licking his face. Aidan adored that spaniel.

The Homer Simpson mug on the side table was a gift from his ex-girlfriend, Kylie. He'd last seen her on his thirtieth birthday four months back, the day she'd dumped him. They'd been dating for some months and he invited her to his home on his special day for "wine with assorted buns and cupcakes and Netflix". He'd got stuck into the food, enjoying himself, but she'd sat with her body twisted away from his and her lips pursed. 'Are you okay?' he'd asked twice, and she'd snapped, 'Fine.' After his fifth bun, she'd jumped up. 'You disgust me. Look at yourself! You suck, Aidan.' She'd waltzed out. He'd felt like hurling a doughnut after her but resisted through timidity.

The shame she'd made him feel that day came crashing back today like a wave. He leaned forward towards the mug. 'I suck, do I?' He grabbed the vacuum cleaner's nozzle, aimed, and switched the machine on. Homer-the-mug vanished with a schwooop. 'Yes!' He turned *EverythingSucks* off, feeling a sense of—what was it?—power. How thrilling! A plan began to form in his mind. If he could purge the sky of a pestilential cloud and the house of his ex's relics, what else could he rid his life of? He rubbed a tender hand over the vacuum's body. 'You and me against the world, *EverythingSucks*.'

In his dreams, he wasn't stuck in a huge concrete vat, being ignored as he shouted, 'Help'. Instead, he soared through the soft indigo night, riding a cosmic vacuum cleaner.

The next day, Aidan woke up with a compelling idea. Around 10 AM, he visited his workplace, carrying *EverythingSucks* in a holdall. No one worked here on a Sunday. His pass let him into the building and he puffed upstairs to the empty office. He was a call-centre operator who flogged things people didn't need to those who bought through habit or boredom: penguin patio lamps, porcelain fairies, garden gnomes with Boris Johnson faces. Aidan's lip curled in disgust as he imagined the junk amassing in houses across Britain.

He stared at his desk. Unlike fellow workers, Aidan had never personalised it. There were no cheeky selfies, no "I'm-a-kid-at-heart" toys. After lifting *EverythingSucks* from the holdall, he set it down on the carpet. He aimed and flicked the switch to Extrapower.

As the desk lurched through the air, Aidan flinched. It got stuck in the nozzle, then crumpled. With a schwoooop, it was hoovered up. His heart thumped hard. *This felt good! EverythingSucks* trembled before he turned it off.

Two Barbie dolls were on Annette Bell's desk. Why would a woman want them? Annette, with her hair extensions and bust-crushing tops, was herself a kind of life-sized Barbie. When he'd asked her out to lunch last month, she'd frowned and said, 'Sorry, who are you?' Was it a put-down or had she genuinely never noticed him? He'd hurried back to his desk, where he'd snapped a pencil in two.

Aidan remembered reading that if Barbie were real, she'd be unable to walk, with breasts that big and ankles that small. 'Eat them,' he said, turning on *EverythingSucks*. The Barbies whooshed into the vacuum cleaner, followed by Annette's desk. Aidan snorted with laughter.

The machine's blue girth had grown several inches, and its nozzle almost doubled in diameter. 'Hold on there, babe. We've still got work.' Back in the holdall, *EverythingSucks* bulged from the top. The bag weighed more than before, but not as much as he expected. He wondered why not.

Aidan left the office, adrenaline coursing through his veins. He headed into town, and halfway down East Street, he halted by the bus stop's "Do Not Smoke" sign. England was full of "Do Not" signs. Why weren't there any "Do" signs: "Do Smoke Here" or "Do A Dance if You're Happy"? He glanced up and down the road, checking no one was watching, and slipped out

EverythingSucks's nozzle. The "Do Not Smoke" sign vanished. He clasped the holdall tight until the machine stopped trembling.

Aidan came to the shops. He often bought lunch here and sat on a bench, feeling like he originated from a different universe. *Look at Café Blanc with its trendy, grey-green awning.* Every town had its own Café Blanc now, but Aidan thought longingly of Grease is the World, which used to be here serving the cholesterol pleasures of sausage and chips. He'd tried to have a coffee at Café Blanc once, but there were too many kinds. He couldn't tell a latté from a frappuccino if his life depended on it. As he stood wondering what to choose, two women in the queue behind first sniggered and then sighed. Lowering his head, Aidan had walked out, wearing his shame like a spilt drink.

Today, the only person in Café Blanc was the middle-aged barista at the counter, who smiled. 'What would you like, love?'

His heart thudded so loud he could hear it in his ears. 'I'd like you to get out. I'm about to vacuum this place into oblivion.'

The woman chuckled. 'We'd all like to do that. The wages are rubbish. Seriously, do you want espresso, vanilla latte—'

'Get out,' shouted Aidan.

The woman's eyes grew as wide as a spoon.

He heaved *EverythingSucks* from the holdall bag and dumped it on the floor. 'I don't want to hurt you, just the café. Run!'

She pelted out.

Holding the nozzle with both hands, Aidan switched *EverythingSucks* on to Megapower, its highest suction, and clenched his eyes shut. The surrounding air shook; his hands vibrated; the loud schwoooooooop lasted minutes. Opening his eyes, he saw nothing but an expanse of floor—the tables and chairs were gone. The vacuum cleaner sputtered for several minutes. Now the size of a cow, it was speckled in a cloud of heavy dust.

He turned it off, contemplating the emptiness surrounding him, before pumping his fist in triumph.

Three women outside pressed their noses to the café window, staring at him. *Ignore them*, he told himself, but his gut clenched tight. *EverythingSucks* was too heavy to lift now, so he dragged it behind him using its black hose.

Outside, a man in a shabby trench coat clapped. 'Bravo, mate,' he said. 'You should get a medal for services to the community.'

A pool of people stood behind the man, mouths agape. Aidan felt a jolt of fear, but there was no going back. What next? Ah, Next should be next. He'd loathed that shop ever since Kylie tried to upgrade his comfy old sweatshirts to merino wool jumpers. He marched across the road, and the crowd parted like the Red Sea.

The woman on the till in Next, who had startled eyes, pointed at *EverythingSucks*. 'What on earth's *that?*'

'This is a stick-up... of sorts.'

She held up her hands. 'Wh... what do you want?'

'To hoover up this shop.'

Her look made it clear she thought him mad. 'Let me get the staff out. Please.'

'Do it quickly.'

The woman and her colleagues bounded out like frightened deer.

Aidan turned the vacuum cleaner on to Megapower. The shop's contents trembled, and the air seemed to quiver. Item after item took off, whipped through the air, and was sucked up with a schwoooooop—dresses, trousers, underpants, even a chunk of ceiling and shopfront. The machine vibrated, clanked. A cloud of thick dust coughed from its nozzle, which was now half a metre wide.

Aidan stood on an empty floor, the sun on his face. 'Yes! Yes!' After brushing the flecks of dirt off his jacket, he walked outside, tugging the vacuum cleaner behind him.

The crowd had grown. Trench-coat man was at the front, grin as broad as a river. 'Go on, mate. Suck up the lot. I haven't had this much fun since the last anti-whatever riot.'

Police in uniform pushed their way to the front of the crowd. Images of police stations, handcuffs, and prisons skated through Aidan's mind. *Oh, god.* He'd never had so much as a speeding ticket previously. Through a loud hailer, a voice said, 'This is the police. Put down the gun.'

'It's a vacuum cleaner,' bellowed trench-coat man.

'Okay. Put down the vacuum cleaner.'

Aidan held up *EverythingSucks*'s nozzle. 'Don't come any closer,' he shouted.

'Suck us up. Wonder where we'd end up. Can't be worse than this humdrum town,' exclaimed trench-coat man. He was promptly bundled off by a police officer.

'Put down the vacuum cleaner. Now!'

Aidan thought he recognised that voice with its Irish lilt. Wasn't it Barry O'Bearn, who'd bullied him at school and had later joined the force?

'Barry O'Bearn?' yelled Aidan.

'Yes. Do... I know you?'

'Aidan Peeley. I knew you at Greenstead High.'

The tall, wiry figure of Barry O'Bearn stepped out in front of the crowd and walked forward, stopping opposite Tesco Express. 'Aidan,' he said through the loud-hailer. 'Put down the vacuum cleaner, please. You're a decent bloke. You don't want to do any more harm.'

Aidan's head spun like a washing machine on a fast wash. Barry was an Inspector? The boy who made his school days miserable. 'Do you remember your chant from school, Barry: "Aidan Pee-Pee/Oh so weedy"?'

'I... I don't know what you're talking about.'

What a liar! Barry had chanted that, or something like it, every day at school. Encouraged his friends to do so, too. Aidan's face reddened. 'Yes, you do.'

Aidan threw the vacuum switch to Megapower. Barry hurtled through the air like a human cannonball and vanished up the spout. With a long schwooooooooop, the front of Tesco Express followed Barry.

Aidan's arms shook. *EverythingSucks* rattled, clunked,

fell silent. The size of a small lorry now, it smoked thick black dust from its nozzle. Coughing, Aidan switched it off.

As the crowd stared in horror, a familiar woman dashed out of the remains of Tesco Express, her dress covered with soot.

'Mum,' Aidan whispered.

'Kipper,' she called, looking about. 'Where are you, Kipper?'

'Mum,' he shouted.

She rushed over. A cut on her cheek oozed blood. 'Aidan. Thank God. But Kipper... tied up by his leash outside... gone.'

Aidan's chest tightened. 'Kipper?'

'What's happened?' She poked a finger at *EverythingSucks*. 'And what on earth's *that*?'

'Oh god.' Aidan's breath came in gulps. As well as Barry, had he just vacuumed up his parents' dog, the only being he truly loved?

'What have you been doing, Aidan?' His mum's expression said, 'You must be somehow responsible for this mess.'

A realisation struck, a roar of voices filling Aidan's ears. One thing he had always hated more than Barbie or Barry.

Using both hands, he turned *EverythingSucks*'s large nozzle towards his own face, coughing at all the soot.

'What are you doing, Aidan?' his mum cried. 'Stop!'

'Run away, Mum.'

'But—'

'Just go. Now!'

After barely a moment's hesitation, she took off.

Aidan's gut quivered as he stared down the nozzle's hole. 'You useless bastard.' He reached out a foot to switch the machine on.

Aidan vanished, not with a schwooooooooop, but with a sputter.

EverythingSucks let out a long, mournful belch.

Acknowledgements

I would like to thank Pete at Elsewhen Press for accepting this book for publication. Thanks to Dot Schwarz, Petra McQueen, Ruth Arnold, Helen Chambers, Richard Dunn and various members of Critiquecircle.com for feedback on the stories. Thanks also to Anne Hamilton and Verity Holloway for excellent editing on some stories, and P.R. Pope for final proofreading.

Elsewhen Press
delivering outstanding new talents in speculative fiction

Visit the Elsewhen Press website at elsewhen.press for the latest information on all of our titles, authors and events; to read our blog; find out where to buy our books and ebooks; or to place an order.

Sign up for the Elsewhen Press InFlight Newsletter at elsewhen.press/newsletter

OTHER ELSEWHEN PRESS TITLES THAT YOU MIGHT ENJOY

The Devil's Halo
Rhys Hughes

A light comedy, a picaresque journey – like a warped subterranean *Pilgrim's Progress*.

In death, as in life, paperwork is hell. The paperwork for the recently deceased Monty Zubris needs to be examined and deliberated upon. So, meanwhile, the Devil has consigned him to the Waiting Room of the Afterlife. It is ordered alphabetically, so he is compelled to make his way to his designated zone, which is, of course, near the very end of the chamber. On this voyage of enormous length, he meets various dead individuals, many of whom wish to tell him their remarkable stories.

"Reading is a mesmeric experience, and *The Devil's Halo* is one hypnotic horizon after another!"

– from the Foreword by **A.A. ATTANASIO**

"Only Rhys Hughes could have written *The Devil's Halo*!"

– **IAN WATSON**, European SF Society Grand Master 2024.

"For many years, I have regarded each new book from Rhys Hughes as continuing proof that the universe is a marvelous, exciting and creative place. His work brightens my days, lightens my burdens, and convinces me that I am in the presence of a font of exuberant inventiveness. THE DEVIL'S HALO is no exception, and might very well be in the Hughes Top Five. All the myriad tales of Hell from Dante onward have never charted any territory as gaily bizarre and humanly affecting as this book unveils. As Monty Zubris traverses the ten-million-mile length of Hell's Waiting Room, the reader is treated to posthumous wonders akin to those in Philip Jose Farmer's RIVERWORLD books. If Anatole France, Voltaire, James Branch Cabell and C. S. Lewis had been born in the year 2000, and come of age amidst our twenty-first-century chaos, they might have collaborated to produce an existential odyssey half as wild and unruly as this one. Somewhere in Hell's Waiting Room, Robert Sheckley and William Tenn are reading this book and splitting their sides with rueful laughter."

– **PAUL DI FILIPPO**, author of Vangie's Ghosts

ISBN: 9781915304704 (epub, kindle) / 9781915304605 (236pp paperback)
Visit bit.ly/TheDevilsHalo-Hughes

OTHER ELSEWHEN PRESS TITLES THAT YOU MIGHT ENJOY

MIRRORS *IN THE* DELUGE
RHYS HUGHES

Mirrors in the Deluge is a collection of 32 unrelated stories that take elements from fantasy, science fiction, horror and other genres and give them a lateral shift. Like much of Rhys' work these quirky tales between them encompass parody, pastiche and puns.

The fun, as ever, starts with the title of each story – gently leading an unsuspecting reader into preconceived ideas and expectations; expectations that are soon spun around, turned on their head (or other extremities), and pushed in an unexpected direction. Thus, a saunter merely through the contents page is already a hugely entertaining experience and one more akin to savouring the hors d'oeuvres of a grand feast than consulting a list of shortcuts into a literary tome. In fact, the gastronomic metaphor serves us well here; the courses on offer range from tantalising tuck to a gourmand's repast, but never mere vittles – perhaps the way to enjoy this book is to digest one story, three times a day (four if you're a halfling who needs second breakfast), rather than trying to gorge on all the available delights and delicacies at one sitting.

To complete this gourmet's guide, a tempting sampling of the stories must include: *The Soft Landing*, a unique story told from the perspective of a photon; *Travels with my Antinomy*, how do you solve a paradox when you're part of it?; *Vanity of Vanities*, the internet achieves consciousness and takes over, but with very different consequences than you might imagine; *The Fairy and the Dinosaur*, in which a fairy can't find what she wants for her picnic in the goblin market, is offered cloned prehistoric plums but turns to a time-travelling robot to go back to the age of the dinosaurs and eat an original plum. Other titles to tempt you include *The Martian Monocles*, *The Prodigal Beard*, *A Dame Abroad*, *The Unkissed Artist Formerly Known as Frog*, *The Goat That Gloated*, *The Taste of Turtle Tears*, *The Bones of Jones*, and *The Haggis Eater*.

ISBN: 9781908168757 (epub, kindle)
ISBN: 9781908168658 (200pp paperback)
Visit bit.ly/MirrorsDeluge

OTHER ELSEWHEN PRESS TITLES THAT YOU MIGHT ENJOY

STUDENTS OF MYSELF

RHYS HUGHES

There are few students in my class. When one considers what the subject is, this isn't surprising. I teach myself.

In other words, I impart to my students facts and fancies based on my life and ideas. It's the least popular class in the university and I doubt it will be funded for another term. But none of that is my fault. I wanted to teach a proper discipline such as ecology, but the authorities wouldn't let me. They insisted that I teach myself; and as a result, I do so.

The students are given an assignment. They each have to write a short piece about how I spend my free time. But this is information I've always kept secret. I can't imagine how they're expected to know anything about my private life, certainly not in detail.

Clearly I'm being spied on. Unless it's guesswork?

I read the essays anxiously.

Yes, only some of them have got it right…

"If I said he was a Welsh writer who writes as though he has gone to school with the best writing from all over the world, I wonder if my compliment would just sound provincial. Hughes' style – with all that means – is among the most beautiful I've encountered in several years."

SAMUEL R. DELANY

ISBN: 9781911409793 (epub, kindle)
ISBN: 9781911409694 (112pp paperback)

Visit bit.ly/StudentsOfMyself

OTHER ELSEWHEN PRESS TITLES THAT YOU MIGHT ENJOY

GALAXIES AND FANTASIES

A Collection of Rather Amazing and Wide-ranging Short Stories

ANDY MCKELL

Prepare for the unexpected

Galaxies and Fantasies is an eclectic collection of tales from master-storyteller Andy McKell, crossing genres from mythology to cosmology, fairytale to space opera, surrealism to hyper-reality. What they all have in common is a twist, a surprise, a revelation. Leave your pre-conceptions aside when you read these stories, prepare for the unexpected, the extraordinary, the unpredictable. Some are quite succinct and you'll be immediately wanting more; others are more elaborate, but deftly devised, and you'll be thinking about them long after you've finished reading. These are stories that will stay with you, not in a haunting way, but like a satisfying memory that often returns to encourage, enchant or enrich your life.

ISBN: 9781915304162 (epub, kindle) / 97819153041063 (186pp paperback)

Visit bit.ly/GalaxiesAndFantasies

ABOUT KATY WIMHURST

Katy Wimhurst is a disabled writer who pens short stories about apocalyptic rabbits, cosmic vacuum cleaners, people turning into mushrooms, knitting to oblivion, existential shrugs, and worlds in which chocolate is illegal. Her fiction has allegedly been called 'dark, witty and magical', sometimes even 'absurdist'. Before discovering the silvery steps that led to Elsewhen Press, she had two books of (magical realist / dystopian) short fiction published, *Snapshots of the Apocalypse* (Fly on the Wall Press) and *Let Them Float* (Alien Buddha Press). She occasionally writes articles about magical realism or speculative fiction. In a very past life, she might have studied for a PhD on Mexican surrealism.

She was born in ▇▇▇▇ [date redacted] and now lives near a pretty river in eastern UK. She is tremendously grateful for trees, seahorses, clouds, chocolate, kindness, and Studio Ghibli films. She isn't appreciative of the illness M.E. which she has had for way too long and is why she has to write fiction on an IPad while lying down. She would like to be reincarnated as a cumulus cloud or one of Wes Anderson's dreams.